Kate Margam lives and works in London. She is currently reading Law at the University of London's Birkbeck College. *Poor Kevin* is her first novel.

Poor Kevin

Kate Margam

Library of Congress Catalog Card Number: 98–86425

A complete catalogue record for this book can be
obtained from the British Library on request

The right of Kate Margam to be identified as the author
of this work has been asserted by her in accordance with the
Copyright, Designs and Patents Act 1988

First published in 1999 by Serpent's Tail,
4 Blackstock Mews, London N4
Website: www.serpentstail.com

Set in Adobe Caslon by Intype London Ltd
Printed in Great Britain by Mackays of Chatham plc

10 9 8 7 6 5 4 3 2 1

for my sister, Jenny

one

HE'S A GOOD BLOKE, is Kevin. All his mates say so. Which would make him smile – he likes things to be simple. Solid, reliable, funny Kevin. He always turns up on time and he always makes you laugh. He's one in a million. If he says he'll phone you, he phones. He's a good bloke. We saw each other every Thursday. He never let me down. He likes to talk. But not much else.

We've become friends over the last few months. Not that I've told him, of course. There's only a few clients I actually like. And Kevin is one of them. He makes me laugh.

Kevin is the most eligible bachelor I know – if there is such a thing these days. It's an old-fashioned concept, but it's true. Kevin is supremely eligible. Tolerant, charming, good-looking and solvent. Poor Kevin.

It all started one January afternoon.

It is not long after New Year and I've been on a bender for two weeks. I came back from my folk's place four days ago and half-heartedly opened up shop. There's only been a few through the door. Most people don't really need us when they're ensconced in family warfare. It's when they're back at work, when routine kicks in, that they surface.

It's about ten to three and still light outside. But it's quiet – like a Sunday. There's only Sheila and me here. Normally there's four of us in the building, but the others are drawing out their holidays. I'm looking in my appointment book when I hear voices outside. Sheila knocks and shows him into my office.

I call it an office, but there's no desk or anything. There's a sofa, TV and video, a bed, three armchairs and a couple of tables. I also have a CD player and bookshelves. I find it relaxes people. If they're nervous they can look through my books or choose some music and I'll just sit. And wait.

Kevin doesn't do this. He walks in, smiles and says,

'Hello. Pleased to meet you,' he holds out his hand. We shake.

'I'm very pleased to meet you, too, Kevin. Would you like to sit?'

I pat the back of one of the armchairs and we sit – not exactly opposite each other, nor side by side, but at an angle. I find this is the least disconcerting arrangement. For them.

'So, do you come here often?' Kevin takes me by surprise and I laugh. It would be hard not to. He has crinkly blue eyes and expensive cuddly clothes. A naturally charming man. He looks me straight in the eye.

'Well, what can I do for you, Kevin?' I intone, still locked in eye contact.

'I'm a gigolo,' he says. One side of his mouth is lifted in a half-smile. I just look at him, fascinated. Well, what would you say? He has very blue eyes, like a young Paul Newman. He draws back to take in my whole body. 'Maybe you can help me,' he suggests and lazily stretches out his facial muscles so that he is smiling properly. He doesn't show his teeth when he smiles. It is a compromising grin. It's hard to imagine that some people need help.

'Maybe I can,' I say and grin back. I have the same kind of smile. It's catching.

'Good,' he says. Then he stands up and shakes my hand again. 'Same time next week?'

'Fine,' I say, trying not to look bewildered. We maintain eye contact. I reckon he's about thirty-five, maybe a bit more; five foot ten; stocky build; fit. When he leaves I sit down and laugh out loud. On my own. That's pretty unusual for me.

I look at my appointment book – 5.30pm: Mr. Daniels. Oh boy, has that one got problems. Not the least of which is his insistence on being called 'Mister'. I get the paper and turn to the back page for the crossword. I find it relaxing.

Thursday, 15th January. 3.02pm. Kevin is late. He comes in smoothing his wet hair. He has short, neat hair. I imagine if he let it grow it would be thick and springy. It's grey – well, kind of dark on the top and back of his head and silvery at the sides. Not black, not brown. No, it's definitely grey. That's what gives him his air of maturity.

'Hi, Kevin,' I say and smile.

'Hello,' he puts out his hand. It doesn't seem stiff the way he does it, just human.

'Is Kevin all right?' I ask. 'I mean, would you like me to call you something else?'

'Well, actually my real name is Elvis, but you can call me Kevin if you like,' he does the grin that I remember from last week. Instinctively, I grin back. 'You can call me anything,' he says with the emphasis on 'you' and widens his eyes as if that was something exciting. He smiles again and confidently pats the back of my armchair for me to sit down.

We sit. I bet Elvis is his professional name and Kevin is the name that is true. I prefer the truth.

'You can call me Louise, then,' I say. I resist the temptation to copy his emphasis. You mustn't mock people – you never know when you're going to uncover their insecurities.

'How are you, Louise?' he mocks me. He speaks with a soft Irish lilt which makes everything sound slightly ironic.

'I'm a little tired, but apart from that I'm fine.'

'Business hectic, is it?'

'It's steady. How are you?'

'Me? Oh, I'm fine. Never been better,' he leans back, relaxed. I wonder what he wants.

'Mmm hmm. Good,' I don't say anything else. I am a professional.

'It's raining. I'm a bit wet. Do you mind?'

'Of course not. Would you like a towel?' I keep looking at his mischievous eyes.

'No, no. I'm used to it. I work outside a lot.' I say nothing. It's for him to tell me, if he wants to. There is a long pause. Kevin looks around the room. Then he gets up and walks over to the bookshelves. 'Do you mind?' he turns back to me. I am going to get used to that question.

'Go ahead.' He examines the shelf at his eye level, clocking the titles of my books. He doesn't do it out of nervousness though, unlike most people.

'You like poetry?'

'Some.'

'Who's your favourite poet?'

'That's hard. There are several, I suppose; Yeats, John Donne . . .'

'I'm a poet,' he says, spinning round. 'Does that surprise you?'

'No,' I say after a pause. It really doesn't. He stands there for a long moment looking at me, enveloping me. Then he walks to the door and puts his hand on the handle.

'Next time I come, would you sit on the sofa with me? Would you do that for me?'

'Yes. If you like, Kevin,' I smile my professional smile. He comes over and puts out his hand. I stand up, we shake and he is gone again. The room seems shadowy somehow. It's because of the weather. I turn on a lamp and tick another entry in my book. Easy money.

I work at the clinic on Mondays and Thursdays and they are exhausting days. We try to split the clients evenly but I seem to have had more than my fair share of sad cases recently. So Kevin is a treat. I expect him to start talking soon. Some people like to establish a rapport before discussing their problems. It makes them feel comfortable.

The following Thursday I am really busy – four clients in as many hours, and every one a passion killer – and I'm finally having lunch at 3 o'clock. Prawn salad and mayonnaise in a crusty white roll. Sheila buzzes through.

'One of yours – Kevin – on the phone. Says he can't make it at the usual time – can he come at five. Says it's easier for him.'

'Yes, Sheila, that's fine.'

'I haven't got him down for today, at all. Is this a private arrangement?' I can hear the bristles in her voice.

'No, Sheila. I wasn't expecting him either.'

'Some people think they own the fucking world.'

Sheila is a bitter woman. She's fat and lonely. But it's her own fault. I think she enjoys being bitter.

'Sorry, I should have called earlier,' he says when he walks in. It's been raining again.

'No problem.' He goes straight to the bookshelf this time.

'You don't have a Bible.'

'Yes, I do. Top shelf. The New Testament.'

'Do you read it?'

'Would you like to read it? Now, with me?'

'No. I can't stay,' he turns and looks at me. Those steady eyes again. Mesmerising. Then, 'Do you mind?'

'Why should I mind?'

'I just came to say sorry, really.' I keep looking at him with what I believe is an open expression on my face. 'You see, I've got a confession. The first time I came . . . well, I didn't really come here for . . . you know. I came for a bet.'

He looks embarrassed now, serious, but he doesn't flinch. 'Do you mind?'

'No,' I say.

'But I would like to come again.'

'Fine,' I smile at him. He moves to the door. Then he stops and with his back to me he says,

'I suppose you've heard it all before. I suppose you think we're all pathetic,' he turns to look at me. I shrug. 'Well, if you don't mind, I'll come back at the same time next week.'

'Okay,' I say and smile again. This is hard work. He leaves – this time without shaking my hand.

When he's gone I sit down and think. What the fuck does this guy want? He seems self-assured, cocky almost, and yet he is so bloody diffident. And what was that stuff about the Bible? Some sort of test? I buzz through to Sheila.

'Sheila, that last one – Kevin. Did he pay?'

'Oh yes, sweetheart. Full whack, no questions. And he shook my hand. Last time, too.'

'Thanks,' I go through to the bathroom and get my things. I don't know why but Kevin makes me feel nervous. Like butter-flies. Maybe the prawns were off. 'Night, Sheila.'

'Night, love.'

For the next few weeks we slip into a routine, Kevin and me. We sit, side by side, on the sofa – which is not what it's normally for – and he asks me questions. Some of them I answer, like, 'What are your top five films?', or 'Do you prefer cats or dogs?' Or we discuss poetry. He doesn't tell me anything about himself. I figure he is just insanely lonely. But I can't understand it – he's very bright and articulate.

Then, one day in late February he starts to open up a little.

'Will you be cooking pancakes on Tuesday?'

'This Tuesday?'

'Next week. Shrove Tuesday.'

'I suppose so. I hadn't realised. But yes, I probably will. Will you?'

'I don't have any children,' he says.

Now, I am very tempted to say 'neither do I', but that would be a lie and I don't like lying. But we also have a rule which is that we don't tell clients anything about our personal lives unless it's really pertinent. He has put me on the spot – and he knows it.

'Would you like to have children?' I eventually ask.

'Five,' he says, immediately. 'Kids are the most important thing in life. Maybe the only thing.'

Men who haven't got children always say daft things like that. Wait till you're kneedeep in dirty clothes and doctors' appointments and Nosey fucking Parkers who think they know better than you, I feel like saying. But not to him. He looks thoughtful, not sentimental.

'There's still time,' I say, instead.

'Oh yes,' he answers, smiling at me. 'There's plenty of time,' he stands up and winks at me. 'Plenty of time for you, too.'

'Yes. Yes, I suppose so.' He puts out his hand, but instead of shaking it he turns my palm down and kisses my hand.

'Bye for now,' he says. And then, 'God bless.'

I am tickled. And disturbed. You just don't know where you are with this one. It's like he's flirting with me. It's not unheard of. There is a delicate balance in all our relationships. And they can quite easily tip over into something unproductive if you don't monitor yourself.

I think hard through our conversations since he started coming. He has not once given me anything personal to get my teeth into. In fact, it's not like work at all. But now something has changed. Kevin has just started his therapy. Children. Much more complicated than sex. I haven't got much to go on, but I figure one of the strongest possibilities to be bereavement. The early death of a partner can shadow people's lives for years, especially if they are childless. I write some new notes for myself on Kevin's case.

Attitude: likes to be in control
Physical: formal contact only
Background: ?
Hooks: children, writes poetry, the Bible
Poss. loss, death

*

I do cook pancakes – Timmy expects it. He goes to a church school so we observe all the yearly routines. But how pancakes came to be a symbol of shriving oneself I've no idea. Maybe Kevin knows.

t w o

IT IS THE END OF MARCH and the sunshine is fantastic. There are daffodils and tulips everywhere and I feel bright, as if something good is about to happen. I always feel like this in the spring. It's stupid, I know – April and May are usually dismal – but I can't help it. Sometimes I think I am an animal. I shouldn't have been born human at all. I feel like falling in love and having babies. Every year.

Nobody knows this about me. Except Malcolm – that's Timmy's father. He often appears at this time of year. We fuck like crazy for a few days and then he goes again. That's the way it will always be. I've grown accustomed to it. Still it hurts. It hurts every day he doesn't come. And every time he does come it hurts when he goes.

Thursday afternoon – time for Kevin. Then I can go home early. He's my last visitor and his sessions are always short. I'll walk the long way home because it is so beautiful out. Kevin arrives on the dot.

He sits on the sofa and pats the cushion next to him.

'Did you miss me?' he asks. I look at him. He is smiling as if it's a come-on. I throw back my head and laugh. When I sit down we turn towards each other like old friends.

'Louise?' he starts.

'Yes?'

'Have you ever been in love?'

'Why do you ask?'

'I just wondered.'

'Have you?'

'No. No, I don't think so. You can't eat when you're in love, can you?'

'So they say.'

'Would you tell me? I mean, would you tell me if you had been in love?' He breaks all the rules.

'Well . . .'

'It's okay, you don't have to answer. I know you can't tell me. But I think about you.'

'Do you? Why?'

'You intrigue me. I think you always will.'

Then Kevin goes over to the table and puts some music on – Viennese waltzes, for God's sake.

'Do you like this? I like this. Shall we dance?' He doesn't really expect an answer. He starts waltzing with an imaginary partner. He shuts his eyes and every now and then he opens one to squint at me and then pretends he's caressing his partner. It makes me smile. When the music pauses he trips himself and sprawls on my floor. He makes me forget myself – I laugh and laugh. I've never had such fun with a client. Kevin lies on the floor and he laughs, too. He looks up at me.

'I like it when you laugh. Promise me you'll never stop laughing. Would you do that for me?'

'Okay, I promise.'

'Do you mind?'

'Mind what?'

'Me? Do you mind me? My behaviour?'

'No, Kevin, I don't mind.'

'I bet you don't laugh with most of your clients, do you?' He gets up now and sits in one of the armchairs looking at me keenly, his blue eyes holding mine. 'What do you do with them?'

'What do you think I do?' I have stopped smiling now.

'Do you enjoy it? I mean, is it just a job or do you ever like them?'

I like him. I do like him. But I don't like prurience. Vicarious thrills are not part of my expertise.

'I don't think about it, Kevin. Do you?'

'I would never judge you, you know. For what you do. It's your decision.'

'What do you mean?'

'I mean whatever you do. It's your business. You're the one who has to live with it.'

'Kevin, do you really think you want to carry on coming to see me?'

'Do you want me to go?'

'It's up to you.'

Usually I wouldn't care, but I don't want to be judged by Kevin. There is a long silence. I shouldn't let him disarm me like that.

'I'd better go now. But I will come back. Will I?'

'It's your decision,' I say, mimicking him. He leaves quietly. I am disappointed with myself and with him, which is unprofessional. I must remember. I must stay ahead of the game.

I say goodbye to Sheila and walk home. I can't get him out of my mind. I've obviously got him wrong. He says he's never been in love. He's interested in me and what I do with other men. He's been manipulating me. Maybe I'm just not cut out for this job. I often think that when I'm making no progress. It's ridiculous really. But Kevin winds me up with his trite little comments.

On Friday a man arrives at about mid-day with a bouquet for me. I am picking up some files for a meeting with Nicole. The card says, 'Sorry. Kevin.'

I'm at the front desk when the delivery man comes in, so I see the look of disapproval on Sheila's face as she hands them over to me. If I hadn't been there I wouldn't have put it past her to bin them.

'What's wrong with that?' I ask defensively when the man has gone. She harrumphs and sucks in her cheeks. She'd be really pretty if she wasn't so fat. I take the flowers into my office.

It's a rather ostentatious bunch. Too much to have them all in here. I've only got one vase and it usually accommodates a single rose or a handful of freesias. I get some scissors from Sheila's desk and dismember the fancy wrapping. There's cut-flower food and all. He must have an in-store account. I wonder if he does this often. I wonder who else he has to apologise to. Then I scold myself for wondering. Kevin is just a client and he will tell me in his own time.

The flowers spend the afternoon in the bathroom, taking up the basin and eliciting envy from the girls. The thought of them makes me smile – maybe I didn't get it wrong after all. Maybe Kevin does genuinely need some help. I mention him to Nicole, the Clinic Director. She thinks it shows appreciation – for a client to send flowers. He's such a gentle person, I'd like to help him.

I am going to make the most of this weekend. Timmy has said he'd like to go kite flying. I'm crap at it, but I'll have a go and probably some man will come over and take charge. Helpless women and children bring out the best in weekend fathers. They're always divorced. The married ones stay at home, I guess.

When I get home, laden with flowers and a Chinese take-away for Timmy like some flamboyant prodigal, there is a surprise for me in the familiar shape of Malcolm. I haven't seen him since before Christmas. He's got rid of that ridiculous moustache, he says he has money to burn and he's staying for a fortnight.

I left my appointment book in the office, but I mentally scan the pages, trying to remember how busy the next week is. Who can I cancel? It's bad practice, but we all have to live a little.

Timmy is, of course, over the moon and monopolises Malcolm until bedtime. Then we sit down with a bottle of wine and a tape of schmaltzy Romanian folk music he picked up in a tube station. He's a sucker. That's one of the reasons I love him.

One of the other reasons is his attitude to my job. It amuses him. No jealousy, no hang-ups, just frivolous scepticism.

'So how are The Impotents?' he asks.

'Still paying.'

'And still impotent?'

'Apart from the three who ravished me this week.'

'That's good. Success at last.' We both laugh. I don't discuss anyone seriously with him. It wouldn't be fair. But sometimes it's hard. I'd like to tell him about Kevin to get some male insight. But I wouldn't know how to start. When I think of Kevin I smile and Malcolm would pick up on that.

So, instead we talk about his work. Malcolm is a spy. Well, that's what I think anyway. Officially he works as a translator on diplomatic missions to the Middle East. And I'm Sigmund Freud.

Anyway, he's been in Dubai for some time and when he takes his clothes off I am shocked again by the contrast of his frazzled neck and forearms against the unearthly white of his torso. I find it deeply attractive – the macho outer image and the pristine, youthful truth. He's very strong, Malcolm. That's another thing I love about him.

I wake up about 10am. Malcolm is still asleep and I go to the kitchen to make some coffee. The flowers are still in the sink with dirty plates piled around them from last night's take-away. I get my big earthenware jug and try to arrange them. I'm no good at things like that. I get impatient.

Coffee, the newspaper, Saturday morning radio and the man I love. These moments are precious to me. I have to make them last for months afterwards.

I'm sitting in the kitchen staring out of the window. The weather is not so good today. It's bright, but in that artificial kind of way with the threat of a downpour gathering strength over the whole of England. No wind. I don't know what I'm thinking about but Malcolm suddenly kisses the back of my neck which sends a tremor across my scalp. Then he places both hands on my breasts and presses firmly, pulling me back against the chair. He leans over my head and kisses my forehead and my nose. I can't bear to be teased. I twist round and pull his body into my face. I kiss his stomach and lick his navel. Malcolm has boxer shorts on and I get hold of the elastic with my teeth. His penis springs up to meet my touch as Timmy walks in.

'Oh God,' he says. He's old enough to be embarrassed.

Malcolm pulls away and stands with his back to us, looking out of the window.

'Well, it doesn't look too promising,' I say, nodding towards the window.

'Mmm,' says Malcolm.

'Oh, Mum,' Timmy whines. 'You promised.'

'Well, we'll give it a go, but don't blame me if we get soaked.' We sit together and breakfast – the happy family. Three or four times a year we get to do this.

Malcolm drives in silence to Hampstead Heath in the hire car – a kind of Jeep. It's so high off the ground you have to climb into it. Perched in the front, looking down on the other traffic, I feel privileged; smug. I don't have a car – on environmental grounds – but I do love the luxury of being driven around. Travelling across London on the tube makes me claustrophobic. Too much proximity.

There's a limp little breeze and a couple of times a sudden wisp gets the kite up and soaring for a matter of seconds which delights Timmy. But it's not a success. We abort at half-past one and zoom up to Highgate for an evocatively drab pub lunch. This is one of the things Malcolm loves to do when he's in England.

Malcolm is trying to persuade me to take Timmy out of school for a few days so he can spend some time with him. I'm not going to do it. It's not long till the Easter holiday. I reckon, if his son is so important to him, Malcolm should be able to rearrange his work schedule to be here. Of course, it's not as simple as that. But it would be if it was me. Everyone would expect a woman to put her family first, jeopardise her career if necessary. But nobody expects it of Malcolm. The disturbing truth is that I don't really expect it, either. It would be nice but unexpected.

He brings it up again when we're in bed. We have a stupid argument during which I say too much. So Malcolm gives up, faking sleep until sleep descends. Which leaves me alone with my fury.

I get up and go for a short walk. It's raining. I make it once round the block and pick up the early Sunday paper at my 24-hour newsagent. I often do this when Timmy is tucked up – Saturday nights are not my favourite time.

So, I'm sitting at the kitchen table, soul music on the radio, reading the film reviews, eating sliced peaches from the can and smoking when Malcolm comes in. These things are a feature of single womanhood and being caught concentrating on them is shaming. I wipe my mouth, push the peach tin away as if it is complicit somehow in my lonesome habits and take a long drag on my cigarette, pretending to be contemplative.

'I don't think it's working.'

'What?'

'This. It's not working.'

'What do you mean?'

'I think I should go.'

He is already half-dressed. He disappears for a few minutes and then stands in the doorway in his coat.

'Tell Timmy I'll pick him up at mid-day. I'll take him somewhere.'

'No.'

'Yes.'

'But . . . this isn't right. You can't.'

Malcolm sighs. 'I'm going,' and he goes. Just like that. He goes.

three

I DON'T KNOW WHAT TO DO with this – sudden death – it's a new one on me. I mean, I've met some emotional cripples in my time, but this is my man. I want to talk to him. I want to convince him he's wrong. I want to be given a chance.

I sit, dumbstruck for a while, then I finish off the peaches and make some hot chocolate. Then I open a bottle of wine. What has just happened, for fuck's sake? What exactly is going on here?

I firmly believe that there is nothing which occurs between people that cannot be mended, that between human beings anything is possible and everything is resolvable. But how do you talk to someone who is not there?

I get up and look out of the window. It's still dark but I can see that the jeep has gone. There is no trace of him. I need to read a book. Someone else's articulacy might engage me in the hours between now and Timmy's wakening. And then he'll be here again and he'll have to talk to me. It can still be recovered.

I take a book to bed and fall asleep.

But it is not recoverable. That's clear from the moment he walks in just after mid-day. An unsmiling, dishevelled Malcolm. He obviously has not slept or shaved. He speaks in monotone, one-word sentences and stands with his arms folded; unapproachable. A Malcolm I do not know.

I fuss around Timmy. Has he got some money, his phonecard, his inhaler? Timmy is unaware, excited. His beloved father all to himself for several hours – oh joy. And they're off.

Of all the Sunday afternoons I have spent on my own, this is the absolute worst. This is like somebody else's life. I am unable to concentrate, to sit, to read; nothing comforts me. I am distracted. There is no other word for it.

In the days before we all signed up for stress management, it was a certifiable mental condition; distraction. Something like alienation but also the opposite – it is very personal and very, very connected.

I'm babbling in my head. I must be sickening for something.

I decide to do some work – something that will require of me that I focus my mind. I get out my copy of our research paper. Nicole and I are examining how changes in the employment patterns of both men and women are reflected in their sexual behaviour. But I can't think today. I pick it up, put it down, read the same paragraph several times without making any sense of it and then stare out of the window. The weather matches my dull mood. It's one of those days that should never have started.

When they finally come back I make tea as Timmy babbles on about the ten pin bowling. Must it always be like this; the men taking them bowling, the women preparing the food?

Timmy has to finish his story for Mrs Sunjavi by tomorrow. She is going to enter the best three in a national competition. I believe in Timmy's creative talent. He goes to his room.

'Right, I'll be off.'

'Malcolm, why don't you stay and talk?'

'Because you don't listen.'

'Yes, I will.'

'No. You'll pretend to listen and then you'll talk and you'll know all the answers and we'll be back at the beginning again.'

'I'll keep quiet, I promise.'

'It wouldn't make any difference. Face it, Lou, you don't want a man in your life. It's over.'

'Malcolm, don't do this. It's not over. Talk to me.' He turns away and looks out of the window. It is getting dark.

'Please. Just talk to me.' He turns back and throws his keys in the air, catching them again before heading for the hall.

'Nice flowers.' He opens and then closes the front door.

What the fuck was that supposed to mean? They are nice. And they are clearly not the kind of flowers you buy for yourself. So, that's it. My modern, intelligent, free-thinking man is jealous. How pathetic. And he tries to blame it on me – 'You don't want a man.' Well, if a poxy bunch of flowers is all it takes to turn him into Fred Flintstone, then I'm better off without him.

I peep into Timmy's room. He's poised over his desk, chewing a pencil, staring at his poster of Prince Naseem. Strange choice of muse.

Malcolm comes and goes a couple of times during the week and I am steadfastly polite to him. He doesn't crack. But it has to be a temporary stand-off. I can't believe this is really the end.

When Thursday comes I thank and scold Kevin for the flowers. If I told him they'd got me into trouble he'd laugh. But I can't. So, instead we discuss his plans for Easter.

Kevin is going to visit his parents for Easter, as he always does.

'We're a big family. Everyone comes home for Easter, and Christmas and the odd birthday. Family is very important, don't you think?'

'Oh yes. In all sorts of ways. I love going home to see my parents. They pamper me. It's a kind of retreat.'

'Is it? I've never thought of my family like that. We've just always done it. I hope we always will.'

'Do you have lots of brothers and sisters then?' He nods.

'Cousins, nephews, nieces. Oh yes – the lot,' he does his satisfied, homely grin. 'All the eldest girls are called Mary and every other boy is a Kevin. It can get confusing.' He scratches his head and winks. 'But I never forget the kids' names. They come over and set up camp in the barn. I spend most of my time with them. They love it.'

'It sounds like fun.'

'It is. When I have kids, they'll come too. It's a good place for children.'

Kevin stretches his arm along the back of the sofa and leans in, facing me. 'Have you ever been to Ireland?'

'No. I don't know why. It seems a long way.'

'Oh it is. Not in spatial distance, though. You travel through time when you go back to Ireland.'

'I always imagine it as a calm place, with wise old men who sit in the pub all day.' Kevin laughs at me. 'Isn't it like that?'

'I suppose it is, compared with London anyway. But I don't know if the old men are any wiser.'

'But they do sit in the pub all day?'

'Well, the women have to get them out of the house somehow, don't they?' I laugh and Kevin beams triumphantly, as if he had hit on a home truth. 'You should come one day. Come to Ireland. It would suit you.'

'Why do you say that?'

'It's different. Like you.'

'And you?'

'Me? Oh, I'm happy wherever I am. I'm always happy. I just go home to do my duty, the good son. And to go fishing.'

'Fishing?'

'Don't worry,' he groans. 'It's not as barbaric as you think and I always throw them back,' he says, rolling his eyes. I'm not sure whether he means it.

'Do you go alone?'

'Sometimes. My mate was supposed to be coming with me this time. I booked three days off work after the bank holiday and now he's gone and let me down. So, I guess I'll have to go on my own again or not go at all,' he pouts like a child.

We're getting on well and I'm actually learning about him, so I decide to risk a probing question.

'Why not take your girlfriend?'

'She wouldn't enjoy it.'

'Have you asked her?'

'No, but I know she wouldn't. Girls don't like fishing.'

'Don't they?'

'Well, it just wouldn't seem right.'

'Mmmm?'

'Okay. Maybe I wouldn't enjoy it if she was there. It's a man's thing, fishing, isn't it?'

'I don't know, Kevin, is it?'

'Well, would you want to go fishing for three days?'

'I don't know, I've never thought about it.'

'You could come with me.'

'But I'm a woman, Kevin.'

'I know,' he blushes ever so slightly across the cheekbones. 'I know you're a woman . . . a girl . . . but you're different. It would be all right with you. We could have a laugh.'

'And why couldn't you have a laugh with your girlfriend?'

'Oh, I could,' he gives me an impish look, his blue eyes unwavering.

'Just not fishing, that's all.'

End of conversation. Kevin is often suggestive, but never crude. Not with me, anyway. Not yet. Maybe he needs some dirty talk. Kevin gets a book down and starts reading aloud. Donne. He reads well.

' "Twice or thrice had I loved thee,
Before I knew thy face or name;
So in a voice, so in a shapeless flame,
Angells affect us oft, and worship'd be . . ."

'This is good. Would you let me borrow it?'

'Kevin, you have no idea how many books I've lost that way,' I sound tight-arsed.

'You won't lose this one. You trust me.'

'Do I?'

'Yes.'

'Of course, you can borrow it,' I sigh inwardly. Sometimes I wonder why I'm doing all this. Will anything ever change?

Kevin picks up on my thought immediately.

'I will bring it back, Louise. Don't you believe me?'

'Of course I believe you, Kevin.'

'I'm not like other men. I thought you knew that.' He makes for the door.

'Kevin?'

'Yes?'

'I do believe you.'

'Oh,' he looks disappointed. 'Is that all?'

'Well, what do you want?'

'I just thought maybe . . . maybe you'd changed your mind.'

'About what?'

'Fishing. You wouldn't come with me?'

'Kevin . . .' God, he is exasperating.

'I know. You can't. Even if you'd like to.'

'You know I can't. Even if I'd like to.'

'Yes, I know.' He opens the door, 'Thanks for the book.'

'That's okay.'

'But you would have liked to, wouldn't you? Just a little bit?'

'Kevin . . .'

'I know. I'm going. God bless.'

Alone, I get out my notebook. Kevin has told me more about himself in this session than in the whole of the three months he's been coming. He has a girlfriend. Still no mention of sex, but what he has expressed quite clearly is a desire to keep her at arm's length.

The easy assumption would be that he is concealing homo-sexual feelings from himself – he has a girlfriend because he wants to conform, but he doesn't actually want intimacy with her – but I am not in the business of making assumptions. And anyway, there's a distinct sexual frisson between Kevin and me when we talk. Perhaps it is time to get someone else in.

Life is not good. At the weekend I try once more to talk to Malcolm. He's not happy either, I can tell. But he will not budge. It's cold and depressing and my life seems mundane. I'd rather be anywhere than here.

When Kevin comes in the next Thursday I feel almost envious of his certainties: his family, his religion, his bachelorhood.

'Will you be going to Church tomorrow or Sunday?'

'I don't actually belong to a church, Kevin.'

'That doesn't matter. Most people don't.'

'Will you be going to church?'

'Of course. I've just come from there now – Maundy Thursday – and I'll be back later this evening. But I wouldn't expect anyone else to. It's just what I like to do. I like to be with other people. To share the moment. You can't deny it, Louise, even if you're not religious there's something special about Easter, isn't there?'

'Maybe . . .' I've never been inclined to join in ritualised sentiment. It leaves me cold. But Kevin's eyes flash at me with an express challenge.

'The idea of resurrection. It's a new beginning, isn't it? You can call it spring or rebirth, whatever you like. Most of the Christian ceremonies are based around pagan festivals. So there's something for everyone.'

'Even for me?'

'Even for you, Louise.'

'You make it sound inclusive, your experience of religion, quite open.'

'Why shouldn't it be? We're all God's children.'

'Yes, I suppose we are. Even if we don't believe.'

'It makes no difference. It's a personal choice. The lads at work think I'm nuts for taking the time off. They're all working, bleeding me dry as it happens.'

'I don't really know what you do, Kevin.'

'Didn't I tell you? Building. I run my own construction company. I advise, make plans, talk to architects, try and make a profit. I'm basically a builder. I'm sure I told you that.'

'No, I don't think you did.'

'Oh well,' he shrugs innocently. 'Anyway, none of them goes to church. But I bet you they'll wake up feeling a bit happier, or more positive this Sunday. I bet you will too.'

'Maybe.'

'Maybe you won't. I don't know you. But I know them and they definitely will because I'll be paying them double time.'

He makes me laugh, Kevin. He's so intent on being acceptable; Mr. Average. And he looks pleased when I laugh.

'I decided I'd go fishing on my own in the end. It was all getting far too complicated. My girlfriend thought it was odd, though. She thought I'd cancel when my other mate pulled out.'

'Maybe she thought you might want to spend your holiday with her.'

'But that's not the reason I booked a holiday. I can see her anytime.'

'That makes it sound rather predictable.'

'Does it? Yes, I suppose it does, but what can I do? I hate surprises.'

'Why?'

'I don't know. Blame my mother,' then he walks over to the window and looks out. 'I would have liked you to say yes. That would have been a surprise. If you had I would stop coming here as a patient. I wouldn't embarrass you. I know you can't socialise with your patients.' I don't say anything.

'It would have been a surprise, Louise. But it would have been okay, with you. That must mean I like you, mustn't it?'

he turns and grins at me, but he is jangling the change in one of his pockets.

I am really too emotionally weary to be dealing with Kevin right now. The last thing I need is a client with a crush on me. It makes them so vulnerable. I wonder if he needs psychoanalysis, not just sex therapy.

'Kevin, I'm going to suggest something which may sound strange. But I want you to know that I believe it would help our progress.'

'Oh, I thought we were making progress,' he winks. 'Not fast enough for you, eh? I'm sorry, suggest away, Louise.'

'I think it would be useful if I invited another therapist, a colleague, to come into our discussions sometimes. Not to judge either of us. Just to be another ear.'

'Safety in numbers, eh?'

'It's nothing like that, Kevin. But I do feel that you might benefit from having another person to bounce off. Widen your options.' Kevin is looking at me. It is a while before he speaks and then he speaks carefully.

'Whatever it is that has happened to you in the last week, Louise, it is not my fault. I'm sure you and your boyfriend will work it out, but you won't be using me as your whipping boy. I am still going to come and see you because I think you're better than this. I had to apologise to my girlfriend yesterday because you made me realise I'd been using her. I hadn't been honest with her. Don't do the same to me.'

And before I have a chance to answer, he leaves.

A pretty speech. It's probably a good sign. Resentment is a stage that someone like Kevin needs to go through before he can really come to terms with the nature of the therapist/client relationship. I find this is often the case with single men. They protect themselves. As I pick up my notebook Sheila buzzes me.

'Yes?'

'I've got Kevin here. He'd like to come back in. All right?'

'Yes, Sheila. That's fine.'

I stand behind a chair. Kevin walks in looking sheepish. He closes the door and stands still, looking at the floor.

'Kevin, I'm sorry. It was just a suggestion. Maybe I put it badly.'

'No, no. It's me who should apologise. I don't usually behave like that. I really am sorry, Louise.'

I smile at him and nod towards the sofa. He hangs his head like a child and comes over to sit with me.

'We haven't got very far, have we, Kevin?'

'Haven't we?' I look at his face. He looks away and smacks the back of one hand, then rubs them together and sighs deeply. 'No. No, we haven't. It's my fault, Louise. I . . . I haven't really been very straight with you, have I?'

'Haven't you?'

'No. No, I'm sorry. I don't know much about this kind of thing. I . . . I don't usually talk about myself.'

'Well, maybe we should start again. Sort out a level of talking that you feel happy with. It's up to you, Kevin.'

'I thought you could help me.'

'But I don't know what the problem is.'

'Yes you do, Louise. You've known all along. Don't think I'm going to fall into that trap.'

'What trap, Kevin? I'm not setting a trap.' Kevin looks at me closely.

'Maybe you're not. Who am I to say?'

'You have to tell me what you want, Kevin. Why you came to see me in the first place.'

'I thought you could have worked that one out on your own, Louise. Why do people usually come to you?'

'Usually, men come to see me because they are experiencing a sexual problem. It's a brave thing to do. It's a difficult thing to talk about. I don't underestimate how much courage that can take. But in the end it's for your benefit. I am here to help. To try.' He doesn't speak, just stares steadfastly at the floor. 'Do you have a sexual problem, Kevin?' I ask gently.

He shrugs.

'It's what I'm here for.'

'I know, but I can't talk to you about that. It's . . . well . . . it's . . .'

'What, Kevin? What is it?' He sighs and rubs his hands on his legs.

'Well, it's private.'

'Yes it is. That's why it's easier sometimes to talk to someone like me. To a therapist. In confidence. But if you won't talk to me, Kevin, there's nothing I can do.'

'No. No, I do see that. It's not your fault.'

There is a pause. I am waiting for him to say something decisive. He doesn't. He gets up and walks round the room, as if he were doing an inventory of its contents. Then he stands in front of me and shrugs. As if it's me who should say something.

'Stalemate, then,' he says and smiles. 'Same time next week?'

'I'm going to ask one of my colleagues to come in, Kevin. Dr Padremans. She's very understanding.'

'I'm sure she is. Have a good week, then. God bless.'

Kevin blows me a kiss as he leaves.

I lie back on the sofa and close my eyes for a moment. I'm tired of work. Next I have the most intractable of cases to deal with. Simon is an insurance agent. He's been coming to me for five months now. It took him three sessions to get his kit off and another two to masturbate in front of me. When he did I had no option but to refer him to a plastic surgeon. He will not go.

In me, he has found a woman who doesn't shriek with horror at the self-germinating possibilities of his inverted erection, and he likes it. Nothing will induce him to undergo surgery. He has accepted that I can do nothing more for him, but not that that is the end of his therapy. He likes me.

Usually, clients with physical disabilities are the most straightforward. But this one is not gratifying in the least. He has dumped his inhibitions all right, but the process has turned him into an exhibitionist; a freak who actually enjoys the perverseness of his own shortcomings. I doodle for a bit in my appointment diary and then heave myself off the sofa to have a fag in reception.

It is with a heavy heart that I talk to Simon about his week. His life is a series of one night stands, which I know is sad and unfair. It's just that I don't like him.

Still, somebody's got to give the guy some relief. So I get down to it. It's part of my job. And I am always most obliging with the clients I have least sympathy for.

Simon deems it necessary to demonstrate again how easy it is for him to get an erection and suggests that if I were to massage his penis in a particular way, with pressure here and here, it might enable him to enjoy himself.

But today, as I exercise my hand and squeeze, gently then firmly, all I can think of is Malcolm. He is leaving for the Middle East on Saturday. So tomorrow is my last chance. That is the real problem.

four

ON GOOD FRIDAY Malcolm and Timmy take a football to the playing fields up the road. I am anticipating a scene when they get back. If Malcolm is really leaving me then I want him to take away all his old rubbish. So I've collected bits and pieces from around the flat and piled them in the hallway. We haven't discussed this. We haven't discussed anything.

But he will have to explain to Timmy who knows something's up because Malcolm has been staying over at our friend Martin's since that awful Sunday. I've fudged it so far by telling him that we had a row and that Malcolm's very stressed at the moment. But I am not going to lie to him.

Skis, tennis rackets, a dusty old case full of papers written in that loopy style that is so familiar to me. I do not want anything that reminds me of the past. The Malcolm Seward that wrote those idealistic essays belongs to a different era. I heave the case downstairs. There is so much accumulated crap. None of which he has looked at in the twelve years since we moved here.

Later, the front door opens, shuts and I hear Timmy run past the things in the hall and straight upstairs to the loo. I don't show my face. I sense Malcolm standing still and quiet for a few moments. Then he opens the front door again and starts moving the stuff down to the car. So that's that.

Eventually he closes the door and says,

'Louise, I can't fit the skis in. You can chuck them if you like, I never use them. Unless Timmy wants them.'

He must know I am in the kitchen because he hardly raises his voice.

'Fine. You ask him, then. And tell him why.'

He doesn't react for a moment. Then he says,

'I think we should tell him together.'

'Tell me what?' Timmy bounds downstairs, still excitable from playing football.

I come out of the kitchen and watch as Malcolm leans against the wall, his face a mask of grim stoicism, writhing internally. He doesn't speak to Timmy who looks up at me expectantly.

'From now on, when Malcolm comes home he won't be staying here anymore. We've decided . . .well, we've realised that we don't want to live together anymore. It's just to do with Daddy and me. He'll still come to see you and take you out.'

Timmy looks at Malcolm.

'Don't you love Mum anymore?' I bite my lip and look at the floor.

Malcolm sinks to a crouching position so he can look into Timmy's face.

'Of course I love her. Just like I love you. But it's not fair on Mummy to have a boyfriend who is always away. It makes it very difficult for both of us. Can you understand that?'

'Yes. But Mum doesn't mind. Do you?' I smile at him.

'I didn't mind before. But people change, darling. We all do. One day we just feel differently about things. Like you do sometimes about your friends. And then you make new friends.'

'Okay,' he frowns, thinking about it. 'But you're still going to come round and see us when you're not working, aren't you?'

'Yes. Of course.' Malcolm is very upset. He is trying to hold it back but there are tears edging their way out of the creases round his eyes. He picks Timmy up and squeezes him hard. He kisses him several times and then puts him down.

'Can I talk to you before you go?' I ask. He looks at me, surprised.

We go into the kitchen and I whisper to Timmy that we'll only be a minute.

'So, you're absolutely sure?'

'Well you seem to be, Louise. Seeing as you've managed to erase every last trace of me from the flat.'

'Why won't you talk to me?'

'Are you going to tell me about the flowers?'

'What?'

'The flowers. I'm not stupid, Louise.'

'Those flowers. Jesus Christ. Those fucking flowers were from a client who thought he'd upset me. They were a gesture. An apology.'

'Well, why didn't you just say that then?'

'Malcolm, I cannot believe that you seriously . . . that all this, this pain is about a fucking bunch of flowers.'

'You see. I don't know you anymore, Louise.'

'You've got another woman haven't you? You've been seeing someone else and you just didn't have the guts to tell me. That's it, isn't it?'

'It's not that simple, Louise . . .'

'Get out. Go on, just go.' I glare at him. He looks broken. He hunches his shoulders and starts to turn the door handle.

'I didn't want it to be like this, you know.'

'Just fuck off. Oh, and Malcolm, when you get bored with her and decide to move on to the next one try not to be such a fucking coward, huh? Try facing up to yourself.'

He leaves, stopping to say goodbye to Timmy again and promising to write to him.

Timmy comes into the kitchen where I have started to peel potatoes. I hope he isn't going to be too upset. I can't hold my own tears in much longer.

'Mum?'

'Yes, darling?'

'Is it okay if I go round to a friend's house?'

'Well, who?'

'I don't know. I'll ring Gerard and see if he's in.'

'Yes, of course.'

'Don't worry. I'll come home for tea.'

'Okay.'

Alone I do not cry. I actually feel quite relieved. I move some things around upstairs to make up for the gaps where Malcolm's books were. I take down the revolting picture his mother gave us which he insisted on hanging in the bedroom and make a mental note to look for something new in Hampstead tomorrow.

So, Easter is a fresh start. Like Kevin said.

five

LISA AND MARTIN are having a party. They're old friends of ours. Well, old neighbours, actually, but when they moved upmarket we stayed in touch. Martin works abroad a lot too, so Lisa likes to drag me along to her social engagements as an escort. I am continuing the tradition by dragging Emma with me tonight. I hate going to parties on my own. Anyway, Malcolm has been staying there so doubtless they know all about it and the last thing I need is sympathy.

We have barricaded ourselves into the only comfortable chairs in the sitting room where most of the party is taking place. Emma is wearing a totally dreamy combination of sheer, flesh-coloured crepe and dark brown brushed silk. She's amazing. She's flabby, reckless and a chronic chainsmoking asthmatic but she looks a million. I am feeling uncomfortable in the bright orange catsuit I decided on at 7 o'clock in near despair. I wanted to look as tarty as possible so people wouldn't feel sorry for me. It shows off my figure but somehow it's just a bit too new, too young looking.

I am talking about Malcolm but Emma is bored. I can tell. She doesn't believe it was ever a proper relationship. She's looking around for a man.

'Last one to pull is an old dog,' I say, before she can get it in and I head for the kitchen where the men will be congregating.

There must be over sixty people altogether. Most of them are older than me, which doesn't make me feel young, it just means there's no talent. In the kitchen, as I expected, I find a collection of eight or so single men who display all the socialising talents of Giant Pandas.

None of them is worth a second glance. I like a good flirt and I have slept with a number of other men over the years, including Martin. I find it's easier to enjoy casual sex if you've got an absent lover in the background. But I've never slept with anyone I'd consider leaving Malcolm for. And now that I'm really single, of course, there isn't a decent shag in sight.

I stop to talk to a gay couple I know who are equally dismayed at the lack of boys. There is one guy, though . . . with his back to me. Tall with a divine bum looking encouragingly indecent in tight leather trousers. He turns at one point and smiles at us. I notice his eyes – they're Continental eyes – very dark and defined as if he had eyeliner on. But the old queens have already spotted him and I hate competing.

I end up standing on the stairs for ages, trapped by a friend of Lisa's with a lisp who thinks I give speech therapy. Unfortunately this is one of those grown-up parties with no music so you're expected to entertain each other with conversation. Which requires a lot of effort and huge amounts of alcohol. So, apart from a vivid moment when Emma rescues me, sits me on the sofa and falls unconscious into my lap, my memory of the rest of the party is pretty shaky.

Which is why when I wake up in a strange bed with a strange man next to me I have this feeling of paranoia. And a thumping headache. My babysitter will be wondering where I am. I look at my watch. It's only 6 o'clock. Time to make an escape.

I get up and locate my clothes, which are neatly folded on a chair, leave the bedroom and search for a front door. In the living room I spy two glasses, an empty wine bottle and cushions on the floor. I honestly cannot remember anything about it.

When I get outside, of course, I have no idea where I am.

I'm wearing this violent orange thing and carrying just a small snakeskin bag with my keys and some cash in it.

I wander up the road in the direction that looks most promising. This is definitely not North London. I can tell by the width of the streets and the buildings which are modern blocks of flats, not houses. East, maybe.

At the end of the road is a huge dual carriageway and it suddenly occurs to me that I might not even be in London. I have to cross the road to read the sign. A11(M) straight on. I'm out near bloody Epping. A phone box; Talking Pages; two cab offices with ansamachines and finally I am rescued by a local minicab which appears to come from the road I have just walked up.

When I get home everyone is still in bed – Sandra, the babysitter in mine. So I make a cup of tea, curl up under the spare quilt on the sofa and try to pull together the fragments of last night.

I wake to the sound of Malcolm's voice talking to the ansaphone. He is leaving a message for Timmy. Nothing for me. I can't be bothered to pick it up.

The next thing I hear is Timmy plunging down the stairs to try and reach the phone before it goes dead. Too late. He replays the message and walks into the kitchen saying 'second week in August' to himself over and over. He'll write it on the calendar. 'Dad coming'.

I must have drifted off again because I come to around one o'clock in the afternoon. Timmy is shaking me.

'Mum, mum. Malcolm's on the phone.'

'All right. Well, you talk to him, darling.'

'He wants to talk to you.'

I heave myself into the hall and mutter something to find myself listening to a strangely familiar voice. It isn't Malcolm, though.

'. . . so I just wanted to check that you got home all right and that you're still on for Saturday.'

'Saturday?'

'Don't tell me you've forgotten already? The theatre? You said you'd like to come.'

'I'm sorry, who is this?' Then there is a pause.

'Well,' he says, camply. 'You certainly know how to puncture a girl's ego.'

'Oh, God, I'm sorry. I'm sorry, I was asleep.'

'That's funny. You were asleep in my bed a few hours ago. Was it my snoring that scared you off?'

Now I pause.

'Look, I'm sorry. It's obviously a bad time, I'll call again.'

'No, don't go. I'm sorry. I really have just woken up. I was feeling a bit, you know . . .'

'Wasted?'

'Yes.'

'Me too.'

'It was a good party, though, wasn't it?' I am stalling.

'It had its moments.'

'Yes.'

'Look, Louise, forget about last night. I don't want to pressurize you, but I would still like to take you out on Saturday. What do you think?'

'Yes. Yes, that would be lovely.'

'Good. Shall we meet at the theatre, then?'

'Yes, yes. Um, which one?'

'Wyndham's. You know where it is?'

'Yes. I'll be there.'

'About seven-thirty, okay?'

'Okay.'

'Bye then.'

'Yes. Bye.'

That's what I call a nice voice – deep and soft. Moments from last night and this morning begin to flood over me: the leather trousers; the pierced nipple – how could I have forgotten? – gorgeous, fluttery kissing round the back of my neck and shoulders in the taxi; sex – good sex – slow, with lots of talking. I snuggle back under the quilt and squeeze my thighs together remembering the way he touched my arse and made me ride on his face. I slide one hand between my legs where I am softly swollen and wet from thinking about him, and drift off into sensuous reverie.

I hear Sandra leave. I am not really asleep, I'm just hiding from Timmy. But after a few minutes he comes in.

'Mum?'

'Yes?'

'It's Easter today.'

'Oh God, Timmy. I'm sorry. I completely forgot. I'll go and get your presents.'

'It's okay, I'll get them.'

'They're in the bottom of my cupboard.'

'I know.'

The rest of Easter day is taken up with telephone gossip about last night's party. Everyone wants to know what happened with me and the leather man. By the time I go to bed I'm beginning to regret saying I'd go out with him on Saturday. Me on a date, for God's sake, like some hopeless, ageing Lonely Hearts loser. I don't even like the theatre.

six

THERE'S NOBODY MUCH booked in at the clinic this week. It's the school holidays. Everyone's too tired and grouchy to think about sex when they're entertaining their children all day. At five o'clock on Thursday Kevin turns up, of course. I've primed Nicole and she gives us a few minutes before coming in.

Kevin takes his jacket off and sits on the sofa, placing a fairly heavy carrier bag on the table.

'That's for you.'

'Oh, what is it?'

'Have a look.'

I open the bag. There is another bag inside but I immediately get a whiff of fish.

'Oh Kevin, it's a fish.'

'Apple for teacher,' he is grinning.

'Did you catch it yourself?'

'Mmm hmm. I saved the best one for you.'

'I thought you said you always threw them back.'

'I lied.'

'Well, thank you, Kevin. That's very thoughtful. Nobody's ever brought me a fish before.'

'I hope you know how to gut it. Have you got a good sharp knife?'

'Oh no.'

'It's okay. Only joking. I did it for you. I left the head on, though. It's the best bit.'

'Really?'

'Yes. I'm a bit of an expert on fish cuisine.'

'I'm sure you are. Look, I won't be a minute. I'll just go and put it in the fridge.'

'Okay.'

I give it to Sheila.

'It's a fish. Don't ask. Can you put it in the fridge for me?'

'It'll make the milk smell.'

'Don't worry. I'll take it home tonight.'

'Yuk,' she holds the dense package away from her, like a lady.

'So, Kevin. Did you have a good trip?'

'Oh yes. I learned a few new tricks.'

'Did you? Good. About fishing?'

'Oh yes. I learned plenty about catching fish,' he winks suggestively. 'What did you get up to?'

At that moment Nicole knocks on the door.

'Come in.'

'Hi,' she says and smiles. Kevin jumps up and holds out his hand.

'It's Dr Padremans, isn't it?'

'That's right. Nicole.'

'I'm Kevin. How do you do?'

'Hello, Kevin.'

'Please sit,' he gestures to an armchair like I told her he would. Nicole moves to the window.

'I'll just sit here, Kevin. I don't want to get in the way.' He waits until she's sitting and then joins me again on the sofa.

'I suppose Louise has told you all about me?'

'Not really.'

'I have this little problem, you see. But Louise is confident that I'll get better soon.'

'Good. I'm sure you will.'

'Kevin, I haven't told Nicole anything about our previous

sessions. I just asked her to come along and be a third ear for us.'

'Quite right too. They can get pretty steamy, you know, Nicole – our little sessions.' Nicole smiles.

'So, tell me about your holiday.'

'Well, like I told you, I really just went to see my family and have a few quiet days fishing on my own. You know,' he smiles over at Nicole. 'A few days away from the little woman.'

'Have you seen your girlfriend since you got back?'

'Oh no. Once a week is enough for me. It's not that serious. Anyway, I thought I'd better come and see you first. Check I'm not doing anything wrong,' he winks at me. 'Louise gives me advice, you know. I'm not very experienced when it comes to romance.'

I don't bother to look at Nicole. I know what she'll be thinking. Kevin is making himself out to be a really gauche, awkward adolescent.

'Anyway, I can't see her during the week because of rugby practice.'

'Oh, you play rugby?'

'Don't pretend I didn't tell you, Louise. She's terrible, isn't she?' He tuts at Nicole. 'She doesn't like me playing rugby because it's so macho.'

'Is that what you think?'

'What, that rugby's macho? But of course. That's the fun. Just the lads, no women around, plenty of rough physical contact. It's healthy.'

'Yes it is. Why did you think I wouldn't like it?'

'Whoops, sorry. Put my foot in it again. I forgot that you're not like other women.'

'Do you feel that your sessions here are useful, Kevin?' Nicole asks. 'I mean, you've obviously got a great sense of humour and that can help – one can't be too serious all the time. But are we giving you what you need, would you say?'

'Actually, Nicole . . . may I call you Nicole?' She nods. 'Actually

I do think we're getting somewhere. I know I might seem like a bit of a clown. I lark about sometimes. But that's only because I find it difficult to talk about things which are so personal.'

Kevin is grinning as if this is all terribly good fun. He's on good form today. He looks at us both quite innocently.

'Would you rather I left?'

'Gosh. I wouldn't want to offend you, Nicole. I'm sure you're a very good person, deep down and a good therapist. But now that I've started – with Louise – I do think that it might slow down my progress. Today, I mean. Being faced with someone new. We are at quite a delicate stage,' he looks at me for confirmation.

'Of course. I understand. Maybe later, if you feel it would be useful, I could come in and have a chat and we could get to know each other a little.'

'Yes, that would be smashing,' he is on his feet ready to shake her hand. 'Well, thanks for everything. Bye.'

After Nicole has left he sits down and shrugs.

'I'm sorry if I dropped you in it, Louise, but I didn't feel comfortable with her.'

'That's okay, Kevin. These are your sessions. It's for you to decide what we do.'

'It's not always that simple, Louise. You have to help me.'

'With what?' I pause. 'Can you tell me?'

'Well, I did want to tell you something, actually. But I don't know if I can now.'

'Something important?'

'Yes. Yes, it is important. I wouldn't waste your time.'

'Would you like to talk about something else for a while and see how you feel?'

'No. No, I don't think so. Not now. It's not right anymore.'

'Look Kevin, I know it's hard for you to say the things that you really want to say to me. But I just don't feel that I can do anything for you unless you open up a little.'

'But I need to trust you first, Louise.'

'Of course. That's why these sessions are in complete confidence. And we'll go at your pace, Kevin. I won't try to make you do anything you don't want to do.'

'Do you know what I'd like to do?'

'What?'

'No, I can't. You wouldn't let me.'

'Well, try me.'

'I'd like to touch you.'

'That's okay, Kevin.'

'I'd like to touch you . . . your breast,' he barely whispers it. 'Would you mind?'

I open my mouth to answer him and am suddenly aware of a prickly white heat freezing my lips and burning in my cheeks. I swallow.

'No, Kevin, I wouldn't mind.'

'I thought you'd say that.'

'Touching a woman's breast is quite normal in an intimate relationship. If that's what you want. I want to help you to be able to enjoy an intimate relationship.'

'Do you think I've never had one?'

'I don't know, Kevin.'

'I touched my mother's breast once.'

'Did you?'

'Yes. That's not normal, is it?'

'Well, it depends. How old were you?'

'I can't remember.'

'What did your mother do?'

'I can't remember.'

'Can you remember anything about it?'

'No.' He looks at the floor.

'That's okay, Kevin. You can talk to me about it whenever you're ready.'

'Can I?'

'Yes.'

'And you wouldn't mind?'

'No.'

'Well, I can't remember much about it because I was a baby.'

'A baby?'

'Yes.' I look at him. 'Oh no, please don't get cross with me, Louise. I was only winding you up. I'm doing everything wrong today, aren't I? Please don't get cross.'

'I'm not cross with you. This isn't a test. I just wonder when you're going to tell me what you want. What it is that you want from me?'

'All in good time. Now, don't forget what I told you about the fish. Leave the head on, grill it fast for about eight minutes each side. No more. Okay?'

'Okay, Kevin.'

'Till next week then. Don't be mad at me, Louise. This is only the beginning. We'll get there eventually. And it will all be worthwhile.'

'I hope so, Kevin.'

'I won't let you down, Louise.' Then Kevin pulls a face that's all lopsided and screwed up with his tongue lolling out of his mouth. It's so absurd and childish I can't help laughing. He seems pleased. 'See. I knew I could make you laugh. Toodle pip,' he smiles and disappears.

'Well, what do you think?' I ask Nicole when we get to the pub.

'I think he's playing games,' Nicole ponders. 'I think he's very intelligent. And attractive,' she pauses. 'That might be his problem, you know?'

'What, you think he has loads of women after him and that causes the anxiety? A kind of intimacy phobia.'

'It could be emotional repression. Being funny may just be a way of fighting off his own insecurity. Depression maybe. Something like that, anyway. Unless he's got a physical problem. But you'd expect him to be more urgent if that was the case. I mean he's been coming for ages, hasn't he?'

'Fourteen sessions.'

'Jesus. That is unusual. Maybe he just fancies you.'

'That's what I thought. You know, he keeps saying that he'll tell me everything one day and that he has to get to know me better before he can trust me.'

'Well, he may be telling the truth. I mean it could be something so simple, but if he's been bottling it up all these years – he's in his late thirties, isn't he? I mean, he will have buried it a long time ago.'

'He talks about his family. That's the only area he seems to take seriously.'

'That's a start, anyway. Well, I think you'll just have to take things at face value for a while, see what you can get out of him. I wouldn't worry too much. But if it goes on for another month or two we should consider switching him over to Emma. I don't want him becoming obsessed with you.'

'I just don't think he'll go to anyone else.'

'Well then, he'll have to go altogether, won't he? If he's not mature enough to handle the relationship. Unless of course, you make some progress.'

'I just think he needs time.'

'Well, give it to him, then. Stop pressurising yourself.'

'Bloody hell, who smells of fish?' George is the landlord of our local. Since going on the wagon he's developed a rude, blustering manner to compensate for sobriety.

'Oh sorry, George. It's me. It's a present.' I hold up the offending bag.

'I could make you take your drinks out to the yard, you know. That's disgusting.'

'Actually, do you want it? I don't know what I'm going to do with it.'

'I'll bin it for you, if you like.'

'Would you?'

'Will I ever? Give it here.'

'Cheers, George.'

We sit down with our drinks and I tell Nicole all about the party and sleeping with this guy, Malcolm.

'Hmmm . . . interesting. The two Malcolms,' Nicole ponders. 'I wonder who was the original. Someone from your past, maybe. A father figure . . .'

'Oh piss off, Nicole. I didn't even know his name. And he couldn't be more different from Malcolm number one. We're going to the theatre on Saturday.'

'Oh, so he's cultured.'

'Yes. Very. I've got to get something classy to wear.'

'Doesn't sound as though he's interested in your clothes, darling.'

'No. No, I don't suppose he is. I don't know. I'm used to one night stands, but not dating . . .' I pause for a moment, horrified by the thought that dating is all I have to look forward to now. 'He seemed very gentle on the phone, you know, kind of normal.'

'Good. You deserve him.'

'Yes . . . maybe I do.'

seven 7

So TODAY, SATURDAY, I leave Timmy in his pyjamas in front of the TV and head for Camden market to look for a new outfit.

I love this place. There's none of that shouting and jostling for piles of knock-off trash, the frenzied scavenging of real markets. Camden is laid back; a parade of beautiful, trendy people; the beat of hip-hop or reggae music and the smell of incense. People come here just to hang out. They often don't buy anything at all but spend the whole day wandering, drinking coffee, eating noodles or chips out of polystyrene cartons or sitting in a cafe with antipasta and just talking. It's a social thing. Especially in the summer.

And they are different kinds of people, too. There are the wandering, drinking, eating people, serious fashion obsessives, ethnic eccentrics and rustic jumper types, bodypiercing and tattoos, textiles, bread, hats and music people. And they all talk. All except the music people, that is. Music people don't talk. They move distractedly, piloted blindly by their own, internal rhythm. I love these people.

I'm a sort of passive eclectic. I relax here. Other people might go to health centres to drink herbal tea or bathe in aromatic oils, but not me. I recommend a weekend observing people in Camden if you really want to unwind and forget about the greyness.

But today I am on a mission. I'm wearing regulation lycra flares, I've got my handbag strung across my body in true paranoid style, replete with cheque book, plastic and a wad of cash. I'm in a spending mood.

Apart from shops and stalls there is something else that Camden has: sex. Lots of it. Everyone is aware of it. It affects the way they move, look at each other. It's a great place to get picked up.

One of the most important qualifications for being a sex therapist is a respect for the act – its beauty, its seduction, its smell, its strangeness. In fact, it's probably a good benchmark for any kind of therapist. Next time you sign on with a shrink, ask them about their sex life (or fantasies in my case), before you listen to a word they've got to say.

At half past two I sit down at a table overlooking the lock with a pint and a bowl of chips, several carrier bags on the floor at my side. I'm letting the sun beat on my shoulders and staring into the vacant offices of a sleek new building on the other side of the canal, when a shadow falls across my table. A voice asks if anyone else is sitting here and I shake my head without looking up. My tranquillity is imperturbable.

But the man doesn't sit across from me, although there is plenty of room. He sits next to me. Quite close. My hand goes to my bag and I squint a look while he shuffles his feet in the cigarette butts under the bench. It's Kevin!

'Kevin, hi,' I nudge him.

'Oh hello, Louise. Fancy meeting you here. Sorry, are you waiting for someone?' He gets up.

'No, no. Sit down. I'm just doing a bit of shopping.'

'So I see.'

'And you?'

'Yes. Shopping.' Kevin stands up suddenly, searching his pockets and pulls open his jacket. 'Oh no, my shopping. I've lost it.'

'Oh, Kevin. You must have left it somewhere,' I look vaguely round the tables. Then he grins and sits down again.

'It's okay, I haven't bought anything yet. I can never decide. Women are much better at shopping, don't you think?'

'Kevin, don't you ever stop messing about?'

'Life's too short to go round being serious all the time, Louise. Don't you agree?'

'If you say so.'

'I'm sorry. It must be annoying for you to bump into me behaving like an overgrown schoolboy, just when you thought you'd left all the nutters behind. Do you mind?'

I laugh at his description of himself. Pretty accurate I'd say.

'No, Kevin. I'm not a monster, you know.'

'Oh good. I didn't know how you'd react.'

'You mean you thought I'd ignore you?'

'Oh, something like that, yes. I don't know. I didn't know if you were alone.' Just then a pretty woman comes over, smoothing her expensive skirt and sits opposite him.

'Hello,' she says to me.

'Hi,' I return.

'Louise,' says Kevin, 'this is Caroline. Caroline – Louise.'

It's only when he sits down that I realise he had stood up when she arrived at the table. Like some sixty-year-old gent. He had actually stood up until she had sat and he'd introduced us.

Caroline seems very nice but I make my getaway after a few minutes. I don't want to embarrass him. I wonder what he'll say when she asks him how we know each other.

I spend about another hour browsing and buying silly things; earrings, a T-shirt for Timmy, candles, joss sticks. I have a frantic, nervous feeling in my stomach all day. Bumping into Kevin, I felt like a schoolgirl who's been caught bunking off. I can't quite believe I am hunting for an outfit to impress, feeling so excited about a date. I don't like it. It's not my real life. Real life is work and Timmy and not a lot else. I'm thirty-two, for God's sake.

People always think because I'm a sex therapist I must be totally cool about relationships. But I'm not. Being a professional doesn't mean you don't go through all the same self-doubt. In fact, sometimes it can be worse, because you can't admit it to anyone. It just means you feel stupid as well. Then you get into self-recrimination. Mind you, that's not necessarily a bad thing. I find the more fucked-up you allow yourself to be, the better therapy you give, because you're exorcising your own angst at the same time.

At home I try to pretend everything's normal. Timmy hasn't mentioned anything although I've told him I'm going out with a man. We've talked about sex before, when he was about eight. And he's used to a lot of his friends' mums having new boyfriends – everyone's divorced round here. But I don't really want to include him in this. Not yet. I don't know what's going to happen. At the moment I think it would be better if nothing happens. I don't want a relationship.

By 6.30 when Sandra arrives I've practically talked myself out of going.

'Wow! You look gorgeous,' she says, making me feel even more uncomfortable.

'Thanks, Sandra. I'm actually going on a date, but I feel a bit stupid.'

'Why? You look brilliant. He'll be gobsmacked.'

'Will he?' I look at poor Sandra. She's going through that awkward virginal phase, wearing sexless, ill-fitting clothes. Too big to be a child but still unformed as a woman. I wouldn't want to be seventeen again.

'What time will you be back?' Timmy appears, doing his responsible parent imitation.

'Does it matter?'

'You will come back, won't you?'

'Yes, of course I will. I might be late, though.'

'It's okay, Tim. I'm staying over tonight,' Sandra is genuinely fond of him.

'Okay. Only don't get too drunk this time.'

'Thanks for the advice, darling,' I smile. He's a funny little man, my son. 'Have a nice evening, you two.'

eight

THE CRUSH OF EXCITABLE suburban tourists in the Wyndham's Theatre is too much for me. I always find the theatre an ordeal. I'm getting some air on the steps when the most good-looking man in the world walks up to me. He's wearing a floor-length leather coat, gel in his hair and heavy black eyeliner. I'm about to be assessed by a man who is far sexier, far more confident and with-it than I am. I feel sick.

He kisses me on both cheeks.

'Hello again,' he breathes in my ear.

I experience something that has not happened to me for a whole week. It's his voice, his breath, his thigh; the nearness of him. In the bloody foyer of a West End theatre, for God's sake.

There's no point trying to be cool. I kiss him on the lips and hold his arm. He is strong . . . tall . . . adult.

'Hi,' I say with a voice that I hope sounds like Kim Basinger. 'You came.'

'Of course. Did you think I wouldn't?'

'I wasn't sure. I know what I've been feeling all week, but I wasn't sure if you felt it too.'

We watch the first half of the play, sexual heat burning through our chairs so that I'm sure the whole audience must feel it. The play is plausible. We clap. At the interval he says, 'Ice cream or drink?' and smiles at me like he's won something.

'Cigarette.'

At the bar I get a few minutes to watch him as a stranger might. He is confident, fit. When he turns round I'd like to be naked. I'd like to unzip his fly and take his cock in my mouth. I'd like to put my hands under his shirt and stroke his hard stomach and chest and tease his nipples with my tongue. I'd like him to ravish me on the floor. Here and now. How to convey that in a smile? He smiles back.

'You don't like it, do you?'

'What?'

'The play.'

I'd like to say that I'd rather be fucking him, but it's a bit crowded in here.

'I wasn't really paying much attention.'

'Me neither. Shall we skip the second half?'

'What?' I've never walked out of a play before.

'I can tell you what happens, if you like?'

'No, it's okay. I think I can guess.'

'It's a happy ending.'

'Is it?'

'To tell you the truth, I've been thinking about something else.'

'Oh yes?'

'Mmm.'

'Me too.'

'Shall we?'

'Where?'

'My place?'

'I have to get back for the babysitter.'

'Your place then?'

'And Timmy?'

'Oh. Will he still be up?'

'It's the weekend.'

'Damn. Back to the play then.'

'Oh no, no. I'd rather just talk. Why don't we have another drink here?'

'I can think of nicer places.'

'Where?'

'A hotel?'

'You're mad.'

'Then I'm in the perfect company, aren't I?'

'Um . . .'

'It'll be okay. I've done it before.'

'I'm sure you have.'

'Well?'

'Okay.'

Reckless.

A short, silent walk.

I try to look disinterested as he negotiates with the receptionist.

'This is going to be a pretty expensive shag,' I gasp as I catch a glimpse of the bill. Malcolm signs it and shrugs, smiling at me. The equivalent of two sessions at the clinic. But then my clients only get handjobs.

'You'd better be worth it,' he tucks his credit card back into his wallet.

'I'll pay next time.'

'Next time?' he looks at me in mock surprise. I wonder what kind of role play I've got myself mixed up in with this man.

A key. A room number. A bottle of wine on its way.

nine

DÉJÀ VU. This is the second Sunday in a row I've been lying on the sofa in the sitting room waiting for Sandra to go and drifting in and out of fantasies about my new lover.

Malcolm is thirty, he's a choreographer and runs his own offbeat dance company. He wears make-up, drinks way too much and talks dirty. I haven't really told him what I do. I don't want to scare him off. It's bad enough being a single mum living in a housing association flat in North London without being thought of as a prostitute as well.

The curtains are shot through with vibrant sunshine bullying me to get up. I should eat. Food suddenly seems urgent. I pull back the quilt and stretch my over-indulged body.

As I'm getting up the phone goes and Timmy yells from the hall, 'Mum, it's Malcolm on the phone. When are you going to get up?'

'Okay, okay. I'm coming.'

'Have you got flu?'

'No, I don't think so. Timmy be a darling and make me a cup of tea, would you?'

'Okay.'

'Hello?'

'Hi. It's me. I just wondered what you're doing now. I'm not doing anything and I thought maybe we could meet, have some lunch, catch a movie, whatever.'

'What, now?'

'Yes. Don't tell me you were asleep again.'

'No, not really. Just dozing.'

'Thinking about anything in particular?'

'Yes, yes I was actually.'

'Mmm. Can I guess?'

'I doubt it.'

'Well, I was thinking about your body,' he speaks slowly, suggestively.

'Which bit?'

'Well, I started with your stomach. I was kissing your skin all over and holding you very close and then I slowly licked all the way down underneath those lacy knickers . . .'

'Mmm?'

'Mmm . . . I can smell your skin. I want you near me now, Louise. I want to touch you everywhere and hold your soft body against me . . .'

'Go on.'

'I want to pull your legs apart and slide your knickers down and gorge myself on your hot beautiful cunt. I can still taste you. Can you feel my tongue?'

'Mmm . . .'

'Are you touching yourself?'

'Yes.'

'I want to get my hands on you. You have the most gorgeous arse in the world. I'm going to lick it and very, very gently I'm going to push my fingertip inside . . . just enough to make you pant. Do you like that?'

'Mmm hmm.'

'Then I'm going to lick your pussy, inside your lips and press my tongue down on your clitoris . . . I'm going to make you come and then I'll reach up inside you with my fingers. I want to see you shiver,' he breathes. 'Does that sound good?'

'Mmm hmm.'

'Would it be all right?'

'Mmm hmm.'

'Can I come round and do it now?'

'Yes please.'

'I'll be there in ten minutes.'

'What?'

'Okay, eight at the most. Be ready,' he rings off. Timmy nearly crashes into me with a cup of tea as I turn in horror to the mirror by the stairs. I am a freak. I haven't had a shower, I haven't even changed. I'm still wearing the sticky knickers and bra he remembers from last night. My hair is a greasy mess and I've got stale make-up smeared all over my face.

'Timmy, quick! Clear up the sitting room for me while I have a quick shower. Stuff the quilt away and make sure everything looks tidy.' I am running up the stairs.

'Why?'

'Just do it, Timmy. It's an emergency. Please.'

The doorbell goes while I am still drying myself.

'Timmy, can you let Malcolm in?'

'Hello, I'm Tim,' I hear him say. I'm at the top of the stairs, rubbing my hair with a towel.

'Hello, Tim. Is your mother in?'

'She's in the shower. Come in.'

'Thank you.'

'Is your name Malcolm?'

'Yes, Tim, it is.'

'Well I won't forget it very easily then, will I? Because my Dad's called Malcolm too.'

'Hey, that's lucky. I haven't got a son, but if I had he'd probably be called Tim.'

'Why?'

'Because Tim's a good name. And anyway, it would be weird, wouldn't it? I like weird things. It would be really spooky if your

Dad was called Malcolm and there was another boy just like you, called Tim and his Dad was called Malcolm too.'

'Oh yeah, wicked. Mum,' he calls up the stairs. 'Weird Malcolm's here.'

'I'll be down in a minute,' I shout. 'Timmy, get Malcolm a drink, will you?' But I hear light footsteps and in a second he is there, wrapping his arms around my naked body under the towel.

'I couldn't wait.'

'I just got out of the shower.'

'You smell like a baby.'

'You've got cold hands.'

'I've got a hot mouth, though,' he is whispering and pressing breathy kisses all over my face. I struggle to look up and see Timmy standing beside us. He catches my eye.

'What do you want to drink?'

'Oh, hi Tim. I was just saying hello to your Mum. Isn't she gorgeous?'

'Yuk.'

'Timmy, why don't you go downstairs, hmmm? We'll be down in a minute.'

'Okay. But you'd better put some clothes on. Because I've opened all the curtains.'

I kick Malcolm in the shin as Timmy turns and heads downstairs.

'Go with him. Be nice,' I say crossly.

'Okay, Mum. You're the boss.' As I turn away he grabs my bare bum and gently bites my shoulder. 'Oh God, I want to get hold of you and . . .'

'Well, you'll have to make friends with my son first.'

'Okay, I'm going. Don't be long.' I watch him walk downstairs, adjusting his trousers. I feel quite shaky.

Jeans and a T-shirt. No bra. There's a slight chill in the air so my nipples are pushing against the stretched cotton of the T-shirt. That should distract him from my bloodshot eyes and the raw stubble rash covering my chin.

'Hi.'

'Hi. We were just talking about you.'

'Oh yes?'

'You've been asleep all morning,' he accuses.

'So what? I work hard.'

'Mmm. And play hard.'

'You look different today.'

'So do you.'

'Yes, but that's just because I haven't got any make-up on.'

'Ah yes, of course,' he scrutinises my bare face.

'But you look completely different.'

'Ah well, that's because I am not who you think I am. It was my twin brother you met last night. But he told me your address and asked me to come round and check up on you.'

'Did he really?'

'Mmm. Remember the birth mark?'

'No.'

'Well, we both have the same identical mark. Look, I'll show you.' He peels his sweatshirt up to reveal a brown mark just above his waist. I don't remember it. But I do remember the nipple ring and I wonder if Timmy has noticed.

'Weird, huh?'

'You're mad, aren't you?'

'Most definitely.'

'That's okay. Mum knows loads of mad people.'

'Does she?'

'Yes, that's her job.'

'I see. Which part of the council did you say you work for?' He is looking puzzled.

'I don't work for the council.'

'Oh, I thought that's what you said. Trying to put me off the scent, huh?'

'No. What gave you that idea?'

'She works with mad people,' Timmy does a gormless expression.

'I see. What do you do to them?'

'I counsel them, as in therapy.'

'Oh I see. That sort of counsellor. Don't mind me, I'm a bit slow. Oh my God. You're not going to start analysing me, are you?'

'That depends.'

'On what?'

'On whether you've got any problems.'

'Well, everyone has problems, my dear. Otherwise life would be terribly tedious.' Timmy makes a face at this. He's not sure how to take the usurper Malcolm.

'You could tell Mum about them. She'll sort you out.'

'I'm sure she will. But I wouldn't know where to start.'

'Mum, Gerard's back today. Can I go round?'

'If he's invited you, of course you can.'

'Can I take some of my rations with me?'

'Yes, of course.'

Malcolm looks at me, puzzled as Timmy races off.

'Easter eggs, from last weekend,' I explain.

'You ration them?'

'I had to. He's got loads of them. The whole family sends food parcels for him. They think he has a hard life.'

'How could anyone think that when he has you all to himself? He's a lucky little sod.' He gets down on the floor and starts kissing my toes.

'Oh God, don't.'

'I can't help it.'

'Well, you'll have to.'

'What would you like to do then?' he asks, leaning on my knees, making me melt. He really has a most beautiful face but he looks paler, more English during the day. 'I bet you haven't eaten. We could go out.'

Timmy reappears, laden with chocolate eggs.

'Right, I'm going round to Gerard's now.'

'Is he expecting you?'

'Yes. I told you before.'

'Did you? All right then. Oh, what about lunch?'

'I made myself a sandwich ages ago, while you were still sleeping off your hangover.' This makes Malcolm laugh.

'Did you? Good for you. When will you be back?'

'Don't know.'

'Well, make sure you're back by six, okay.'

'Okay. Bye.' He turns and looks quite seriously at Malcolm. 'See you, Malcolm,' he says.

'Bye Tim. See you soon.'

Timmy bundles out with his chocolate stash.

'Now, where were we?'

'You were just starting on my feet.'

'Yes, but look at those breasts.'

'Where?'

'Here. Just sitting on your chest like . . . like . . .'

'Like what?'

'Like they need to be sucked . . .'

ten 10

TIMMY'S BACK AT SCHOOL this week and as I've hardly got any Thursday clients left there's not much preparation to do. So, I spend Wednesday cleaning the house from top to toe. Nobody would know that Malcolm had ever existed. But I don't fool myself. I know what I'm doing. I'm seeing a man who makes me feel like a sex goddess, and after precisely twelve days I'm making a nest. It's primeval.

On Thursday Kevin comes in, sits down and looks at me.

'What do you think of consumerism?' he says.

'What?'

'Well, do you think it's right that you can buy anything?'

'Kevin, I really don't know if I have an opinion on it.'

'Yes you do. You know you do. We're supposed to believe that buying things can make us happy. That everything is available if you've got the cash. What do you think of that? I mean, you above all people, must know that you can't buy happiness. Otherwise you wouldn't have all these lonely men coming into your office every day.'

'Well, of course you can't buy happiness. But I don't see that there's anything wrong with wanting a few comforts in life.'

'Of course not. But it's not just a few comforts, is it? Come on, Louise. You know as well as I do that people really think they can spend their way out of any problem. That success is being able to buy a big house and redemption is something you put off. Stick it all on the credit card so you don't have to think about it.'

'That is very profound, Kevin, and I'm sure you're right, but I don't really see what you want me to say.'

'I want to know what you think, Louise. I want to get to know you. You see, I think we would all be happier if we rediscovered some of the simple things in life. The excitement of the first strawberry of the season; catching your own fish – working hard for those things, not just picking them up in the supermarket.'

'But, Kevin, people do work hard. People work very hard all week in order to buy those things in the supermarket, or save up to buy a house or go on holiday. It's just different work, that's all. We're not peasants anymore.'

'You see. I knew you'd say something sensible like that. So now I don't feel too bad about telling you that I didn't really catch that fish for you.'

'Didn't you?'

'No. I bought it in a fishmonger's on the way here. I thought you would have guessed. You don't catch sturgeon off the east coast of Ireland,' Kevin laughs, smugly.

'Oh, I didn't know.'

'No. I went to a great deal of expense to get that for you, Louise. But I wanted to. I wanted to give you something special. But I also did it as a trick, you see.'

'How's that, Kevin?'

'Well, I wanted to see if I could fool you. I wanted to see if you'd guess what I'd been up to. But you didn't, Louise. That's going to be a problem, you know.'

'Is it?'

'Well, it means we're not on the same wavelength yet, doesn't it? It means I'm right, you see and we have to get to know each other a lot better than this. And in any case, how did you think

I kept it fresh all week? Did you really think I carried it all the way over from Ireland in a carrier bag?'

'I don't know, Kevin. I didn't really think about it. You told me it was a gift and I accepted it. Simple as that.'

'But nothing's that simple, Louise. Haven't you realised that yet?'

'Kevin. I am a therapist. I help people who have particular problems. You seem to enjoy coming here just to make jokes and play games with me. It doesn't bother me, after all, you are paying for your sessions. But I wonder why you do it? It's a relatively expensive way of having a laugh.'

'Uh oh. Now I've really done it, haven't I? Now I've really gone and made you cross. You see, that's my trouble, Louise. I never know when to stop. It's only because I want you to like me. But I always seem to go too far. Will you forgive me?'

'If it's forgiveness you want, for whatever reason, Kevin, you're in the wrong place. I don't give out forgiveness. I get paid for the time I spend with you. What happens during that time is up to you. But, I will say that if you are not serious about continuing your therapy, if you just want somewhere to spend your Thursday afternoons then I can recommend a few nice cafes and I could give over your appointment slot to someone who needs it more urgently.'

'Point taken,' he touches his forelock and then grins. 'So, what shall we do today?'

I don't bother to disguise my long sigh as I look at him. He has a twinkle in his eye like a naughty schoolboy. It doesn't matter how irritating he is, I can't help liking him. There is something so innocent, childlike about the way he behaves.

'Kevin, I want to ask you a question, which I think is important for our progress.'

'Okay, fire away. Only don't ask me anything about sex. I'm not sure I know you well enough yet,' he laughs. It's a double bluff.

'Who do you trust?'

'Well, that's easy. My family.'

'Who else?'

'No one. Is that it? Can I go now?'

'Why don't you trust anyone else?'

'Ah. What you really mean is why don't I trust you, isn't it? And I'm not sure I know you well enough to talk like this.'

'Well, suppose I were to tell you that I am almost the opposite of you, Kevin? That I trust everyone. What would you think of me?'

'Well, that's your business, isn't it. I might think that you were a bit of a fool or that you were lying. Or that you were going to get hurt. But it's none of my business, is it? I wouldn't say you were wrong.'

'You wouldn't say it, but you'd be thinking it.'

'Maybe.'

'But why shouldn't I trust people, Kevin? If I am strong and confident in myself, what have I got to lose by trusting people?'

'But you're not, are you? Well, I don't know, maybe you are. But you'd be a very special person if you were strong and confident all the time. I don't think anyone is.'

'But, if no one is strong all the time, if we all have our weaknesses and uncertainties, that's all the more reason for trusting each other, isn't it? If we're all in the same boat?'

'Look, I don't like this conversation, Louise.' Kevin is looking at me with a wide open expression, but he is clasping his hands together, tightly.

'Other people might find it easy to come and talk to you about the most private things in their lives, to trust you with their most intimate thoughts. But I'm not like that. Maybe I'm wrong, but I don't think that's strength. It would be weak of me to tell you everything now, wouldn't it? There'd be no mystery anymore, no surprises.'

He gets up and puts on a pair of sunglasses before continuing with his back to me. 'Yes, we do all have our weaknesses, but I am not about to tell you mine. I pay to come here. But it's not because I think I can buy happiness, or peace of mind by confessing to you. I respect you, Louise, but you're not a priest. Far from it.'

Well, why is it, then Kevin? Why do you come? But he had gone. In a flurry. Not exactly a temper, but certainly bad feeling.

eleven

APART FROM THE SEX, it's a bit like being with a woman. Malcolm talks about himself a lot. He teaches modern dance as well as choreographing new pieces. He used to do ballet – that's why he's got such an exquisite body – but he gave it up a few years ago and says he's much more fulfilled working behind the scenes, creating. We're lying in bed and he says, 'Ask any dancer and they'll tell you. Learning a new piece of choreography is the best sex they've ever had. That's what they use – sexual energy. That's why they're so amazing to watch.'

'That sounds rather incestuous.'

'It is. For the choreographer too, teaching a new step is like having vicarious sex. It's the most exciting thing in the world.'

'Then it's voyeurism.'

'Oh, pardon me. And your job isn't?'

'Touché. So why do you bother having sex at all. I mean, how can you come back to a woman like me when you spend your days having vicarious sex with all those perfect bodies?'

'Well, that's where your job comes in. You see, to understand a dancer, you've got to appreciate that it's an obsession. They live, sleep and breathe dance. There is nothing else. Like all creative people, they have terrible lovelives.'

'Well, now I know you're talking bollocks. I know quite a few creative people who have perfectly satisfactory relationships.'

'Well then, they're superior beings.'

'Like you?'

'Me? Don't you believe it. I've got my baggage, darling.'

'Have you?'

'Yes. But I'm certainly not about to tell you all my secrets.'

'Why not?'

'Because you'll probably decide I'm hopelessly deluded and never want to see me again.'

'Don't be daft.'

'Well, that's what you do, isn't it? I mean, how can you stop yourself? Don't you find yourself analysing your friends all the time? Your relationships?'

'No. Of course not. It's just my job.'

'Anyway, you wouldn't want to know about me.'

'Why not?'

'Because nobody ever does. Or if I do tell them they run a mile.'

'Me too.'

'I don't think so, darling. You said you were with Malcolm for twelve years.'

'Yes, and how much time did he actually spend with me? Anyway, it isn't just him – I didn't say I was faithful to him all that time, did I?'

'So why would anyone want to run away from you?'

'Because of what I do. It scares them.'

'Yes, I have to admit, getting into bed with a shrink is pretty scary.' He does his B-movie shock-horror expression for me.

'See,' I fold my arms, but Malcolm leans towards me and gets serious.

'I like you, Louise. I really like you. And I don't want you to think I'm a freak.'

'Why should I? Because of the make-up? Because you're bisexual?'

'Oh God, did Lisa tell you?'

'No, she didn't. I guessed. It's pretty fucking obvious.'

'And you don't mind?'

'As long as you don't jump into bed with the first tasty bloke that comes along. Or woman for that matter.'

'Just because you like sex with women and men doesn't mean you must be obsessed with it or something. I'm not particularly promiscuous.'

'I was only joking. I'm sorry. It must be difficult. People's attitude to sexuality is tangled up with all sorts of fears and prejudices. Most people are pretty frightened of sex, full stop, never mind what they consider unconventional sex.'

'But you're not.'

'Well, I'm a superior being.'

'Don't hit me for saying this but I have to say, I've always thought shrinks are the most fucked up people of all. I don't know if it's because they have to deal with other people's problems all the time and it sends them crazy or whether they have to be crazy in the first place to want to do a job like that.'

'I don't know either. I do wonder about it sometimes.'

'Do you find yourself absorbing your clients' problems? All their neuroses?'

'Not really.' I decide to take the plunge. 'Most of my clients are men and their problems are very specific,' I say, slowly.

'Why's that?'

'I'm a sex therapist. I deal with men and their sexual problems. Impotency mostly, but that's just the surface problem. I have to get a bit deeper than just the physical.'

Silence.

'Does that put you off?'

'I don't know. I had to go to a shrink once.'

'What for?'

'My mother sent me. He was supposed to be a sex therapist too.'

'What did he do?'

'He tried to put me on drugs.'

'Why?'

'Because I refused to stop wearing women's clothes.'

'Oh.'

'Does that put you off?'

'I don't know.'

'I'm a transvestite, Louise. A TV. How would you treat me?'

'Do you need treatment?'

'No.'

'Are you happy being TV?'

'Mostly, yes.'

'Well that's okay then.'

'Is it okay with you?'

'Well, it doesn't put me off, if that's what you mean. It's interesting.'

'Oh God.'

'Well, doesn't it put you off me, that I spend my life with my hand down other men's trousers?'

'Metaphorically, you mean?'

'No, I don't. I treat people, Malcolm. Whatever they need. You see, I'm like you. I believe you can damage your entire being if you cut off your sexual energy, if you deny yourself. Some people block off their sexuality as a way of repressing things they don't want to face about themselves.'

'And you unblock them?'

'I try to, yes.'

Malcolm looks at me for a while. He pushes my hair back off my face and strokes my cheek.

'You're really special, you know that?'

'Am I?'

'Yes.'

'Why?'

'You're serious about things. You're a serious woman,' he kisses me deeply on the mouth.

'And you're very beautiful,' I say.

'Me, I'm just an animal.' Malcolm pulls back my hair roughly and sticks his nose into my neck taking a long sniff. Then he puts my hand on his erection to show me.

'That's mind over matter,' I say, feeling a deep warm spasm through my buttocks and pelvic muscles. 'I didn't say you don't have an incredible mind.'

'Oh, so that's why you slept with me that night after the party, eh? Because of my mind.'

'Yes.'

'Me too.'

'Oh,' I notice my watch and sigh.

'What is it?'

'I ought to get up soon. Timmy will be back for tea.'

'Don't you dare run out on me.'

'I can't. I live here, remember.'

'Seriously, I mean. Do you promise?'

'You can stay here with me if you like.'

'I can't. I have to get home tonight. I'm rehearsing all day tomorrow and I need my sleep.'

'Now who's running out?'

'I'm not going anywhere yet. And neither are you . . .'

I reluctantly chuck my new lover out just before Timmy gets home.

He's stuffed his face with sweets all afternoon and can't eat his tea, so we watch a video together. I ache all evening.

Alone in the kitchen, I'm wallowing in memory and washing up a few things before going to bed when Timmy appears in the doorway.

'Mum?'

'Yes, darling?'

'Is Malcolm your new boyfriend?'

'Oh, I don't know yet, Timmy. Maybe.' He watches me. 'Timmy go to bed now.'

'Okay,' he doesn't move.

'Timmy, now please.'

'Okay, I'm going. Mum?'

'What?'

'Is he gay?'

'No, darling, of course he's not gay. What on earth made you think that?'

'Nothing. Good. I like him.'

'Do you?' But he's scarpered to bed

And how much do I like him, I wonder. I've always fancied the idea of men wearing make-up – I know plenty who'd look a damn sight better for it – but I'm not sure how I feel about the idea of my lover wearing women's clothes. Have to wait and see, I suppose.

But it's funny. If Malcolm – I mean my Malcolm, ex-Malcolm – had ever met a bloke with a pierced nipple, wearing make-up he'd probably have thumped him. And I liked that tendency. I liked him behaving like a stereotype. But he never made me come like this sex maniac does. And he'd never consider doing anything remotely kinky. I wonder just how kinky things are likely to get between me and my new Malcolm . . .

twelve 12

THE NEXT MONDAY, Henry the actor, turns up with his wife, Petra. He's been coming on and off for nearly a year and doesn't seem to have made any progress at all. He talks a lot of psychobabble which is boring at best and at worst may mean he's in serious denial. But at least he cries sometimes, usually when he is talking about his wife.

She is a successful artist. I've been dying to meet her for ages but she's always jetting off round the world to promote her exhibitions. Henry is forever promising to bring her in as soon as it's convenient, but I don't really believe he's even told her he comes here. So, I'm pleased today when they arrive together.

She is nothing like I'd pictured her. She is small and ginger with a squashed face and layer upon layer of secondhand clothes. She is also very open, which I had imagined.

We sit and talk, the three of us, running over some of the discussions Henry and I have had in the last six or seven weeks. Petra speaks frankly.

'We have been through a lot of these issues before, you know. Like whether I should dress up or learn to talk dirty. I've never been much good at that kind of thing, though. I'm more of a straight to the point kind of person.'

'Well, those kind of fantasy games can make a difference. It's great to be adventurous and have some fun in bed. But only if it is fun. Obviously, the minute you feel any pressure or responsibility to perform something you're not happy with, then you should stop.'

'Well yeah, we did. I mean, I just couldn't really get into it, you know. I get the giggles. And obviously, that doesn't help,' she grins at Henry, a little embarrassed. She obviously cares about him.

'You know, this might sound obvious, Petra, but when a couple first admits that there is a problem, things can get worse for a while. You may start seeing sex as a burden or an obligation and that can make it harder to enjoy, because you're looking for a solution. That can be a big responsibility.'

'Oh yes. Well, I definitely think that's happened to us, don't you, Henry?'

'I suppose so,' Henry is much quieter than usual.

'And it could be that you're looking for a solution in the wrong place. Have you talked about that?'

'What do you mean?'

'Well, it may be that by focussing on your sexlife, you're actually ignoring what's really going on in your relationship, or even outside of it. I mean, you've been together for, what, fifteen, sixteen years?'

'Yes.'

'And over that time, have there been a lot of changes in your circumstances: your work, where you live, who you mix with?'

'Well, yes, of course. I mean when we met I was still at college. We've been living together for twelve years. But then, of course, a lot of that time Henry's been away on tour. And now I'm abroad quite a lot.'

'That must be difficult.'

'I don't know. I suppose it can be. Henry?' Henry looks up.

'Well, obviously it's difficult,' he says, acidly. 'It used to be Petra who was left at home while I went off and now it's the other way round. So now I'm getting a taste of what it's like.'

'What is it like?'

'I've told you how I feel about this before. It's not what you think. I don't resent Petra for going away, for being successful. I'm very pleased for her.'

'Henry, this is not about blame. I know we've talked about it on our own and we can draw a line under it if you like. But I think it would be foolish not to take the opportunity to examine how you actually feel about this, now that Petra's here as well.'

'Well, I feel terribly guilty about it,' Petra interrupts. 'I mean, this year I've been away more than I've been here and I know how awful that can be for the one who's left at home. You always wonder what they're up to; are they having a better time without you, are they getting off with someone else? You can't help it.'

'I do not resent you going away, Petra. I've told you that. I've always trusted you.'

'I know you have, but telling me, or telling yourself doesn't necessarily make it true, does it? I've been trying to make it up to you, being especially nice when I get home, trying to make you feel better. I have tried.'

'Yes, I know that. But it doesn't make me feel better. It just makes me more depressed. Why should you have to worry about me? You've got far too much going on. I should be the one who's being supportive.'

'I think Henry's frightened that I'm going to leave him. He's been out of work for nearly a year now and I've been swanning off all over the place. I know what that's like. It knocks your self-confidence and makes you feel inadequate and then you get angry with yourself. But I've told him I don't want to leave him. There's no way I'm going to leave. We can get through this. We've got through worse things before.'

Henry doesn't say anything. He's staring at his hands. He wants to cry, but perhaps not in front of her.

'Henry, we've talked about this question of confidence quite a lot, haven't we? About how we rate ourselves and rate our sexlives. Low self-esteem, depression, money problems . . .' I look at Petra. She has a receptive face. 'You'd be surprised how many people's sexlives mirror their income patterns. When they're earning good money, the sex is good, and when their income drops, they withdraw.'

'Oh God yes, we've been through a bit of that, haven't we?'

Henry nods.

'I wouldn't have dreamed of coming to see anyone about it though. To tell you the truth I've always been rather sceptical of therapy and counselling, you know. But I'm really proud of Henry for coming. I put it all down to those men's health magazines.'

'There's no need to patronise me,' Henry thrusts his face at her.

'I'm not.'

'Yes, you are. You are. All the time you think you're being understanding and mature about it you are making me feel more and more useless. I need to sort this out myself. I don't want you feeling sorry for me, Petra.'

Petra shrugs and raises her eyebrows at me.

'You're right, Henry. If you're feeling bad about yourself already, it can make it worse when your partner shows their concern.'

'Yes. That's right. I do feel bad about myself. And yes, your concern does make me feel worse.'

'But that's what it is, Henry. It's concern. It's love. You're very introspective at the moment, you're analysing yourself all the time. You can't see yourself as other people see you. But Petra sees Henry, the man she loves, going through a hard time and she wants to help.'

'Maybe it would help if I just cut down on my exhibition work. We could think about starting a family sooner. I mean that's the only reason I'm working so hard,' she looks at me earnestly, justifying herself. 'Because I expect that in a couple of years time, I'll be stuck at home with babies.'

'Don't start that again. It's bloody ridiculous. If you stopped working now, what would we do for money?'

'Well, it's got to happen sooner or later, hasn't it? I can't put it off forever.'

'Had you always planned to have a family?' I ask. This is a new slant on things.

'Oh, we've been discussing it for ages,' Petra starts to say as Henry very loudly says,

'No.'

She never wanted children, she admits, until recently.

'Why now?' I ask.

'Well, I think it's because I'm getting older and I suddenly realised that this is it. In a few years time, I won't even have the option anymore.'

'And this natural barrier, this ultimatum – as you see it – does it frighten you?'

'Yes, definitely.'

'So the sudden desire for children – does it come from that fear, would you say?'

'Well, yes. It's now or never, isn't it? It was different when I was making the choice for myself. Now my body is making it for me.'

'I've had that feeling, that my body is taking precedence over my conscious will. It's quite unsettling. I think it is something most women go through from time to time.'

'Yes. Yes, that's exactly how I feel. It's something I've been resisting for years. But now, it's just there. I can't get rid of it.'

'So you take it out on me. Blame me for not wanting children,' Henry is angry.

'I don't want to take it out on you. It's just that I'm changing and you're not.'

'But I don't think you really are changing. I think you're just frightened. All women get like it at your age.'

'Do you think that's a helpful way of looking at it?' I ask, as gently as I can. I am making notes as we go, trying not to look at either of them.

'I am frightened. That's the whole point. Can't you see? I'm frightened and you're clamming up. It's hopeless.'

'Everyone finds it difficult to adapt to change – in our lives and in our relationships. When we're frightened we often clam up,' I say, head up.

'Are you saying I'm the one who's frightened?'

'No, Henry. Petra has said she's frightened. It's a new situation. How do you feel about it?'

'Yes . . . How do you feel about it?'

Henry stares at us in turn without saying anything for a few moments. Then he stands up and makes a terribly dramatic gesture with both his arms.

'Okay, maybe I am frightened. Maybe I'm shitting myself. Because my wife, the career woman who always said she would never have children, has suddenly changed her mind. And I'm thirty-nine and out of work. How do you think it makes me feel?'

He sits down again. Bullseye.

'Henry, I don't want to sound too brutal, but it could be that you are subconsciously withholding sex from Petra as a way of punishing her for making you feel like this.'

'Yes it could be,' Henry looks at me aggressively. 'It could be that I'm doing that subconsciously. Or maybe it isn't all that subconscious. But that still doesn't help us, does it?'

'Well, of course not. If sex is not the problem. If you're not allowing yourself to get aroused because you don't want to.'

'Maybe.'

'How often do you masturbate, Henry?' He looks at Petra when I ask this.

'Go on,' she says. 'Tell her.'

'Would you say you masturbate more or less since your difficulties with arousal started?'

'I don't know,' he fidgets. 'More, maybe.'

'Mmmm hmm. Do you use magazines, or videos . . . ?'

'Sometimes.'

'Have you ever thought of watching an erotic film together?'

There is a pause as they look at each other.

'We tried it once, but Petra didn't like it.'

'That's because it wasn't erotic. It was just revolting. It made me feel sick.'

'Well, the line between pornography and what is erotic is a completely subjective thing. But there are all sorts of erotica. Why don't you go and choose something together?'

'And then what?'

'And then watch it, Henry, with Petra.'

They look at each other again.

'Okay,' says Petra.

'Well, look, we'll have to end the session there today, I'm afraid. I hope you feel it's been of some use. I think you'll agree, Henry, that your loss of libido is clearly a symptom of other issues between you which you need to discuss. Do you agree?' He nods sulkily.

'And I think you should try and come here together for the next few sessions. But of course, just talking about things isn't likely to make the problem go away. So we need to try and tackle the sexual question separately as well. Here's the card of a video place I use. It's very good. They've got a much better selection than a high street rental.'

'Okay.'

'Okay, Henry?'

'I suppose so.'

'Will you think about what we've said?'

'Yes.'

'Good. Now there's one more thing before I let you go. Whatever else happens, I want you to try not to have sex after the film. Okay?'

'Oh. Why?' Petra is very innocent.

'Just to take the pressure off. For a while. For an experiment. Don't expect things to change overnight. Will you try?'

'Yes. Okay. But what if, you know . . .' Petra looks at him.

'What if I get aroused?'

'Then you can just enjoy getting aroused together without the pressure of having to make love, okay? It could be fun, you know.'

'Okay.'

'Will you come and see me together again? Next week?'

'Yes. Yes, we will.'

This is what makes it all worthwhile. Moments like this. When the pattern is broken. This is why our kind of therapy works. We do intervene. Most decidedly we do.

I sit on Sheila's desk to smoke – the reception area is the only place it's allowed – and think about what to do next with Henry and Petra. I may be getting nearer to the root of his struggle. It is not about sex. That much is certain. He had no problem getting an erection the first time he came to see me. It's more like a kind of depression. I may need to refer him. He might respond to anti-depressants. But it is very difficult to get men to face the possibility that they are suffering from a mental illness. Even a mild one.

Next in is Mike. He's a lovely, pretty young man who gets so wound up about sex he either ejaculates before he's got his trousers off or can't manage it at all. He hasn't had a proper relationship yet and he is nearly twenty-five.

It's early days in his treatment. I am teaching him how to relax and breathe properly so that when his erection happens it doesn't seem so uncontrollable. If he manages not to ejaculate before he touches himself then I'm trying to show him how to touch his body, to sensitise other areas. It's a fairly traditional approach, but he is so emotionally fraught, it is proving to be slow work.

After Mike, it's good old Mr Daniels who comes in about once a month to watch a video and masturbate in front of me. And then he always asks me to help him. I hate him. He's some kind of lawyer and he speaks to me as if I'm his private nurse. Which I suppose I am in a way.

We've got a clinic meeting. These are monthly sessions where we raise concerns, argue about how much money we can afford to pay ourselves and Sheila winges on about us nicking her pens. But they are useful for discussing tricky cases. Sometimes we send Sheila out of the room – it is not necessary for her to know everything about the clients.

Emma wants someone to come in on her first session with a fifteen-year-old boy who had a testicle removed after a football injury. His mother is paying and doesn't want to leave him alone with Emma, but obviously we can't have her sitting in with him. So I volunteer.

Then I mention Henry.

'It's the same old lesson. We've made progress for the first time and all because he brought his wife in. You just cannot tell how much of the story you're getting if they keep coming on their own.'

'But we have this discussion over and over, Louise. We can't force them to bring their partners in. They'd just stop coming and then we'd lose all our business.'

'I know, I know. But there must be some better way of advertising, so that we get the message across.'

'But we've got plenty of clients.'

'Yes, and plenty that we get nowhere with because they will not let us. It's frustrating.'

'Well, what do you suggest?' Nicole asks.

'I don't know. I'm just fed up with jerking off sad old men who are too self-important to go to a brothel where they belong.'

It's not like me to get so angry. I know what it is. I'm falling in love.

And it's making me queasy – putting out for all these strangers when I should be keeping it for my man.

'It's a professional hazard, darling,' Emma points out, unre-assuringly.

I stay at the clinic till late, listening to Beethoven and writing up some notes when Nicole comes into my office.

'What are you doing still here?'

'Catching up,' I groan.

'You're bored, aren't you?'

'Oh, not really. Well yes. I suppose so.'

'How do you fancy coming to the prison with me tomorrow?'

'Really?'

'Let me check with John. I'm sure he won't mind. Just to observe.'

'Oh, God, I'd love to, Nicole.'

'Okay.' She goes off to make the phonecall.

thirteen

NICOLE VISITS THE PRISON most Tuesdays. It's her pet project. She works with sex offenders. Rapists, violent abusers of women and children, men who have committed incest, usually with several members of their family. All men. Many of them were abused as children themselves. They are all near the end of their sentences and Nicole's workshops are part of a rehabilitation programme to get them ready for life on the outside. Mostly they are terrified, she says. Not just of being outcasts – victimised – but of themselves; their potential to re-offend.

Nicole has been developing this project for a couple of years now. She finds it the most fascinating and challenging of all our territory. But she has to be careful to keep the two strands of her caseload separate. Otherwise you start seeing psychoses in everyone.

This week there is an addition to the group – a convicted paedophile – who has just been transferred here from up North. I recognise his face from the news a few years ago. The media went to town on him. The regulars are finding it hard to accept him into the group so it becomes a fairly traumatic session.

X (as he appears in Nicole's notes) looks fairly normal in the flesh. A bit crumpled, but nothing like the thuggish identikit sketch I remember from the newspapers. He doesn't say anything. Just keeps his head bowed while the others mumble curses and spit on the floor near his chair every now and then. Three prison officers have come in with him and they are standing at the back, vigilant.

Nicole introduces me to the group as her assistant. She asks them to tell me a little about themselves. I am shocked by how precisely they talk about their offences. Not in gruesome detail, but carefully, so that I understand just how despicable each and every one of them is and perceives himself to be. It's eerie, this communal confessional. Voices functioning, but without drama, as if they were removed from the whole experience. The opposite of our normal clients who are completely eaten up by their own personal failures.

When it is X's turn to speak he doesn't open his mouth, just twitches a couple of times.

'Sick cunt,' somebody whispers. A few of them mutter through clenched teeth. 'Fucking kill the bastard,' and 'You're dead.'

I look at X – a modern leper. I wonder what it must feel like to be him. Somebody the world hates. Someone who will never be forgiven. He just sits there, trapped in his own person.

Nicole asks if someone would like to explain why they are all feeling so aggressive. Nobody speaks.

'Maybe you're right to feel like this about X. Maybe what he's done is evil.'

Somebody grunts. But nobody looks up.

'Well, of course it's easy to pick on someone you don't understand, isn't it? We all know about that.' There is a bit of shuffling.

'So, perhaps we should discuss what we think evil is. Where does evil come from? What makes someone evil? Is it the same thing that makes someone behave badly, do something that he knows is wrong,' she says after a long pause.

'If you can't tell the difference you're as fucking sick as him,' Ted is the most eloquent. He's a big black guy and the others defer to him on account of his size. But he's in here by accident. He's always maintained he was fitted up and Nicole believes him.

'What difference?'

'Oh come on. Doing that to a kid. Hurting a fucking kid. That's sick. It's depraved. He's a fucking animal.'

'Does anyone agree with Ted?' They all nod. The paedophile doesn't move a muscle. He is a small, broken man.

'Okay, so everyone agrees. So can we change someone like this? Is there any value in the rehabilitation process?'

'No way, man. He's just gonna do it again and again. It's in his fucking head, man. He's sick. No way you're gonna change him.'

'Well, I might say that everyone in this room has done something evil. Everyone's done something that society says is sick and evil. So can anyone change? James, what about you?'

James looks up. He's a thin, white pasty-looking man who assaulted three women at knifepoint in a single week. He stares at Nicole for a few moments, then he suddenly lurches out of his chair.

'Whore. You're a whore. A fucking whore,' he splutters and tries to make a grab for her. Ted is there before the warders. He pushes James to the ground, then turns to start on the paedophile. There's a messy kind of scrum as the guards get stuck in and Nicole rushes over to the intercom to get more help.

Eventually, we are let out of the room as more burly officers bundle in. James and X are removed and we are allowed back in to continue the session. A kind of grim hopelessness has gripped them now. It seems to inhabit the room, dictating the demeanour of the men; more pathetic than threatening.

'They shouldn't of let him in here, man. No way. He should be in a fucking asylum. And they shouldn't ever let him out.'

'Please excuse James's behaviour,' a man I had not noticed before speaks. He has a cutglass accent and is smiling at me benevolently. 'He has a young daughter. He misses her. It's understandable.'

I smile back politely. My brief is to watch and keep my mouth shut. Nicole turns to the one who just spoke to me and asks him to continue where we left off. Richard is – or was – a doctor who fondled a few too many of his female patients. He talks about his past as though it were unproblematic. 'I did that. I'm not proud of it. I regret the hurt I caused.' It is his future that is the problem. Where will he go? He has lost everything and everyone who ever loved him.

I find myself becoming wrapped in the same heavy morbidity as the men. Prison is like a space somewhere between life and death. You exist but without any social being. It is definitely oppression, but I cannot quite see how it benefits anyone. Maybe if I was one of their victims I'd see it differently. I listen to their halting efforts to discuss something which must seem unreal to them; the outside world. And it makes me see the inevitability of them re-offending. As if this experience is merely a disjunction and when they get back out there, they will revert to their previous incarnations.

At the end of the session we drive back to the clinic in near-silence.

Nicole takes me to the pub where I sink half my pint without looking up.

'Well? You're very thoughtful.'

'God, where do you start?'

'I felt like that at first. But I think I'm beginning to understand more now.'

'Fucking hell, you touched on some really raw stuff, Nicole. I wouldn't dream of talking to our clients so roughly.'

'These people are beyond the pale. Outcasts. Society will never accept them however much they change. There's no point pretending it's all going to be easy.'

'Jesus,' I shake my head. It's hard to imagine what will happen to them. 'Is it always like that? I mean when that guy went for you, you seemed so cool.'

'What could he do? If he really tried to hurt me, they'd kill him.'

'Yes,' I take another long drink, thinking. 'Isn't it weird how they seem to think it's okay to abuse women, but not children?' I think again. 'Or maybe that's not so unusual.' I look up at Nicole. She is smiling at me.

'I'm glad you came, Louise. I'm thinking of applying for funds to turn over part of the clinic for a kind of halfway-house, a day centre.'

'Really? What do you think the enlightened residents of historical Hampstead would have to say about that? I mean, they wouldn't approve McDonalds because of the kind of people it might bring with it. How on earth would they react to a bunch of cons; perverts?'

'Well, that's just one of the problems. How to keep it secret. We'll have to sell it to the police and the local authority, of course. But they've been good to us for the last ten years.'

'Yes, but our clients are all white and middle class. And that's another thing. Have you thought how they might respond – forced to mingle with a bunch of sex offenders?'

'Different days of the week. It would have to be.'

'God, I don't know, Nicole. I agree it's important, but it's a big move. You couldn't do it on your own.'

'No. That's why I'm asking you.'

'Me?'

'Yes. I can get you on a training course with the one and only residential centre in Britain. If you're interested.'

'God, Nicole. Let me think about it.'

'Of course. We'll talk again next week. Have a look at that paper I wrote last summer. That'll give you a broad idea of the scope.'

fourteen 14

I TAKE TIME TO READ through Nicole's prison reports over the next few days. It's good to have something to get my teeth into. I find I'm much happier when I'm working hard. Timmy spends most of the weekend in the park, roller-blading with Gerard. The boots cost me a fucking fortune, but he's getting plenty of entertainment out of them. I seem to have been indulging him more and more since Malcolm's exit.

My man is rehearsing all weekend and I probably shan't see him until next Saturday. But he is mature enough to phone me several times to let me know he is thinking about me.

It's the last week of April and the weather is turning continental. By Thursday it is hot, hot, hot. Kevin is due. He comes in at 5pm, looking serious and ever so slightly damp on the forehead and temples. But clean, of course. He sits on the couch. I sit on an armchair.

'Hello, Kevin,' I smile. He says nothing, but looks at me. I wait. He is not smiling, not blinking. 'Are you well?'

'How long is this going to go on?' he asks, still looking at me.

'That's up to you.' I had hoped he would be in a better mood this week. I want to bring Nicole in again.

'I don't know what else to do, Louise.'

'Well, what do you want to do?'

'I want to make you laugh.'

'Mmm?'

'Is that so terrible?'

'Of course not.'

'Shall I tell you a story?'

'If you like.'

'Will you listen?'

'Yes.'

'It's about my parents.'

'Mmm hmm.' Nicole will be waiting for me to buzz her. But I will listen to what he has to say first.

'Last year was their fortieth wedding anniversary. Can you imagine that, Louise? There aren't many couples who stay together that long, are there?'

'Not anymore, no. But I think it's fairly common for our parents' generation. I suppose people's priorities have changed.'

'Not mine. I think when you find the right person you should stay together, whatever happens. Most people don't wait though, do they? They jump into bed with the first person they fancy and then they've got nothing left to give when the real thing comes along.'

'Is that what you think, Kevin?'

'Yes, don't you?'

'I don't know. It depends on your beliefs, I suppose. Some people might say that sharing an intimate relationship can enrich your life without being so exclusive.'

'Yes, but that's just an excuse. I don't mind if people want to be promiscuous. But they should be honest about it. Real love is different though. If you don't save yourself for it, you'll never know.'

'Yes. Some people do say that.'

'It's true, Louise. It was true for my parents, anyway. My father waited until he was thirty-two before he married my mum. And they've been together now for forty-one years. And that kind of stability is what gives children the best chance. Don't you think? Knowing that they've got a family behind them all the time and that will never change.'

'That's an ideal, Kevin. But it may not be realistic for many people. Most people, maybe.'

'Well, maybe I'm not most people. Children are the most important thing in your life. If you have them, you should be prepared to give up anything for them. I think it's sad the way so many children are forced to come home from school to an empty house and wait all alone for their mothers to get back from work. Don't you think that's sad?'

'Not necessarily, no.'

'I'm not saying I blame people. I know how hard it is to keep a mortgage and a family going. People have to work. But then, maybe they should wait before they have children.'

'Life is about compromises, Kevin, isn't it?'

'I've never compromised. I wouldn't ever leave my children alone, at risk from who knows what. Am I being too critical, Louise? Do you mind?'

'Of course not.'

'I mean, I wouldn't know anything about your arrangements, or how you would behave if you had children. I mean, it's none of my business.'

'That's right, Kevin. Now, before we go any further I wonder if you'd mind Dr Padremans coming into our session again. It would be just like last time. She won't interfere.'

Kevin gets up and walks round the room with his hands in his pockets. He doesn't say anything.

'Kevin?'

'Yes?'

'Would that be okay with you?'

'Whatever you say, Louise. Go ahead, buzz her.'

I pick up the phone and ask Sheila if she can get Dr Padremans for me. Nicole knocks and comes straight in. Kevin is standing with his back to the bookcase. He moves forward and puts his hand out, but he doesn't smile at her.

'Good afternoon, Dr Padremans.'

'Good afternoon, Kevin.'

'Please sit down,' he pulls a chair round for her, in the far corner of the room, where she sat last time, but facing the sofa which he then sits on. He starts talking again, more formally, as if we are his audience.

'I was just telling Louise about my parents' fortieth wedding anniversary last year. I think it might help to explain something about me. You see, I'm keen to move on with my therapy.' He looks at Nicole who smiles.

'They had a big party at the house. Everybody came – it's a close community at home, not like London. Everyone knows everyone else. Actually you can't keep anything private. That's one of the reasons I wanted to get away. As you know, I'm a bit hung up about people knowing my personal affairs,' he does that self-deprecating grin I know so well.

'The whole family was there, all the children, aunts, uncles, cousins, in-laws. Everyone and the priest. My mother was dressed up. She looked smashing. I mean, for an old woman. She's kept her looks, you know. It was a good crack,' he smiles, but the monologue is stilted, uncomfortable.

I smile back.

'The kids were playing around, you know. And the oldest bunch, Gemma, Mick and the two Maries, put some music on and did this dance. Even my father enjoyed himself. He doesn't drink normally, you know, but he'd had a couple of glasses of champagne and so had my mother,' he pauses and runs both hands through his hair, loosening his neck muscles. I've never seen Kevin so tense. It shows another side to him, a troubled side.

'It sounds lovely,' I am actually quite touched that Kevin is talking like this.

'It was. It was a good party. You know, a family party. I like that, don't you, when people support each other. They're simple people, you know? Do you mind me telling you this?'

'No, Kevin. I'm interested.'

'Are you? Anyway, Dad got up and said he'd like to make a speech. My dad doesn't talk about himself much. He's a gentle, quiet man. So everyone settled down and he told us about how he met my mother. They knew each other from school, but my mother lived in the next village. One day he went over there to help with some work on the church. My mother was in there arranging flowers and when he saw her he said she had a halo over her head. It was the light coming in through a small window. And he said she looked like the perfect virgin, so he asked her to marry him.'

'How romantic.'

'Yes it was. And the way he told us. He looked so proud. My sister, Mary, the oldest, started crying. Then my dad proposed a toast to my mum.'

'That's a lovely story, Kevin. I can see why you are so close to your family.'

'I haven't finished yet,' Kevin leans forward and takes my hand and holds it for a moment. I don't do anything.

'Then my Mum says she's got a story as well. And she sits there, next to the priest and tells us that the night before their wedding she slept with my father's brother.'

'Oh, my God,' I gasp, despite myself.

'Then she goes on. She won't shut up. She says that she's been having an affair with him for forty years. She turns to the priest and tells him that it was because my father wouldn't have sex with her. They never had sex, Louise. Can you imagine that?'

'Kevin. I'm so sorry.'

'I don't want you to be sorry. I want you to try and understand.'

'Well, what did your father do? What happened?'

'Nothing. Nothing. He just laughed and said she was having a joke.'

'And was she?'

'No.'

'Oh.'

'So you see. I am not my father's son.'

'No. I see.'

'It's all a mystery, Louise. That's what he was saying. Life is a mystery and you never know the truth.'

'Mmm.'

'You don't know the truth about me, Louise.'

'Don't I?'

'No,' Kevin gets up to go. He touches me on the shoulder.

'But one day, if you want me to, I'll tell you.'

'Okay,' I look up and smile at him. He suddenly breaks out into an enormous grin.

'Keep guessing, Louise. Next week I promise to make you laugh,' he chucks me under the chin as if I were a child.

'Okay, Kevin.'

'God bless,' he says. Then he turns towards Nicole and executes a strange little bow. 'Goodbye,' he says politely and swings out of the office.

After a pause I shrug my shoulders at Nicole who smiles.

'Strange man,' she offers.

Nicole suggests that Kevin is simply experimenting; playing out different poses to try and find a way of talking without being embarrassed. I'd figured the same, but still I can't help getting frustrated at myself for not having drawn him out more. She tells me to be patient.

The girls persuade me to go for a drink and then start grilling me about Malcolm. Emma pretends to be envious, but then Emma could have any man she wanted – if she ever really wanted one.

I leave the pub about two hours later, feeling guilty at leaving Timmy with the babysitter again. She's a nice girl, Sandra, but admittedly rather dull. I know Timmy feels he has to sit and talk to her. He always complains that she doesn't let him watch his favourite programmes.

When I get home they're eating ice cream in front of the telly. I give her the money and see her out. It's dark and turning cold again. As she walks down the road something catches my eye and I turn and peer in the other direction. A man is just turning the corner, hurrying. He looks familiar somehow – the shape of him.

I close the door and stand for a moment, trying to place him. It's weird but I've had this sensation a few times recently. As though someone is watching me. But I can't quite get hold of what it is. It's like a mild panic. I must be feeling guilty about something.

'How was your day?' I ask Timmy.

'Fine. How was the pub?'

'Good. We had a laugh. Do you want to do something this weekend, go somewhere?'

'Will Malcolm be coming?'

'I don't know. What would you like to do?'

'Dunno. Go shopping?'

'Shopping? Well, that's not very exciting. What do you want to go shopping for?'

'I want to get some new computer games.' They'd bleed you dry, kids.

'But, darling, I bought you those roller-blades a week ago. I haven't got any money left.'

'Doesn't matter, I've got some.'

'Where from?'

'Dad.'

'Timmy, has he been here?' I immediately suspect that my earlier paranoia may not have been unwarranted.

'No.'

'Are you sure?'

'Yes. God, Mum. I'm not that dopy. I would know if my own father had been to visit.'

'Well, where did you get the money from then?'

'He sent it to me.'

'When? I haven't seen any post for you.'

'I'll go and get the letter if you don't believe me.'

'What did he say?'

'Nothing much.'

'Did he say when he's coming over?'

'He's coming in August. I told you that ages ago. It's on the calendar.'

'Yes, all right, I know that. But did he say anything else? Did he say he'd be coming over before then?'

'No.'

'Are you sure?'

'God, Mum. Sure I'm sure.'

'All right. I just wondered, that's all. So, you want to go to Oxford Street, huh?'

'Okay.'

'Okay, we'll go on Saturday. You could ask Gerard to come if you like. We'll have lunch and go to the cinema afterwards. Okay?'

'Yeah, cool, Mum. I'll ring him now.'

Could it have been Malcolm that I saw, spying on me? Why would he do anything so sinister? Maybe he's having regrets. Maybe his new woman has dumped him. That's a very satisfying thought. Maybe she's been having affairs with all his friends and he's feeling betrayed and lonely. Tough shit.

fifteen

WE'VE AGREED TO GO OUT tonight – Saturday. I don't know what I should wear. What do you put on when you're going out with a transvestite for the evening? Do I compete? Or should I try and dress down? I know I shouldn't feel that it complicates things. He's just being himself. I should be myself.

It is beautiful out. I hustle Timmy and Gerard through the crowds on Oxford Street. They gossip quite contentedly and spend over an hour picking their way through CD-Roms, videos and God knows what else in the Megastore, like men twice their age. Always at the back of my mind is the problem of an outfit. I can't quite picture it.

About three o'clock I can't stand it anymore. I dump them in Leicester Square with some money for the cinema and their tube tickets home and whizz off to ransack the clothes shops in Hampstead. I've got no cash left, but I have got a credit card. The ingenues are out in force, spending Daddy's money and hanging out in cafes with unsuitable foreign boys. I don't envy them. Well, only their bank accounts.

It is a single-breasted mock tortoiseshell bootleg trouser suit. It has to be. £229 including a sequined boobtube. It feels right. I sit, satisfied in Haagen Dazs and make myself feel sick for another £6. I've got good vibes about tonight.

A bath, a duty phonecall to my mother and I've been ready

for ages, listening to music, drinking and smoking. To get myself in the mood. The doorbell rings and I saunter through to the hall.

'Hi.'

Into my flat walks a man – at least he's not wearing false boobs – in a wraparound Mexican print skirt and a rough silk waistcoat thing. Oh, and carrying a small leather handbag.

'Hello gorgeous,' he kisses me on the cheek and then wipes the lipstick mark off with his thumb. I stand back to let him in.

'Ready?'

'Yes. I was just having a glass of wine.'

'I wouldn't say no.' As he comes through to the sitting room I remind myself that this has taken more courage from him than it is going to take from me.

I pour him a drink and when I turn round to hand it to him I can't help laughing. He is sitting in the armchair and his skirt has fallen away from one knee because he can't keep his legs together.

'Hussy.'

'Thanks,' he grins and pulls at his skirt. 'Cheers.'

'I'm not sure about the boots.' They are perfectly nice brown leather ankle boots with a Cuban heel but there is a gap of a couple of inches between them and the end of the skirt.

'I know, but I couldn't get one long enough and I just had to have it,' he says, tugging at the skirt.

'It's an unusual print. Where's it from?'

'Camden.'

'No, I meant . . .'

'Louise, we're not going to talk about clothes all night, are we?'

'Sorry.'

'Look, it's not an endurance test, you know. If you don't feel comfortable with it, we'll stay in instead.'

'No way. I'm looking forward to it.'

'Are you?'

'Yes. Let me just get my bag.'

But Malcolm has started rolling a joint when I come back in with my bag, so we have another glass of wine and smoke it. Immediately all the tight connections in my head and body gently fizz away and I hope we're not going places where I ought to be coherent.

As we step outside the flat I have to ask,

'Are you sure it's going to be all right?'

'What do you mean?'

'Well, you know. Is it safe? You know what some people can be like.'

'Oh that. Well, I was hoping you'd protect me. Seeing as you're the one wearing the trousers.'

'Be serious. It's Saturday night. All the lads will be out on the piss.'

'Why do you think I wore a skirt that opens? I'm a mean kickboxer, you know.'

'Are you?'

'No. Well, not yet, anyway. But I had a class today.'

'Why?'

'For the new show. I'm supposed to choreograph some authentic streetfighting. It's very exciting.'

'I must come and see it.'

'You'd better come. You're my inspiration.'

On the tube we get a few looks, but nothing too unsettling. In fact, several women glance at Malcolm and then smile at me in a conspiratorial way. As if it's all a big joke. It probably is. I smile back indulgently, aware that my face is hanging heavily on my skull. It's been a while since I had decent grass.

I watch Malcolm from behind as we travel up the long escalator at Leicester Square. He still looks gorgeous from the back. You can see his broad shoulders and muscly arms and the shape of his cute bumcheeks through the skirt. Other people look as well. When we get to the top I grab him and give him a kiss on the lips, just so everyone knows.

'Hey, queer boy,' someone shouts as we make our way up to the street.

I carry on walking, but Malcolm turns and stops.

'Problem?' he asks, equally aggressively.

'Hey, keep your skirt on, man.' His friends seem to find this incredibly funny. They're just a bunch of teenagers, black guys hanging around the tube station with nothing to do.

'Yeah, funny,' Malcolm turns and comes up the steps towards me. One of the boys spits at him and it lands just by his foot.

'Fucking queer.'

'Oh, get a life,' Malcolm says as we come out into daylight.

'God, you were cool. I'd have thumped the silly runt.'

'No, you wouldn't. Not with all his mates there. But if we see him again on his own . . .' he smiles at me and takes my arm.

'Where now?'

'Old Compton Street of course. I'm taking you to my favourite bar.'

The place is thronging with tourists and gorgeous men in pairs. Hardly anyone glances at Malcolm's clothes. I guess he feels safe here.

We sit in a cool bar at a table for two and Malcolm orders a bottle of wine. Well, he doesn't so much order it as flick his eyes at the barman who comes over a moment later with an ice bucket and two glasses.

'Do you come here often?' I ask, mystified.

'Every now and then.' The barman is a flawless, bleached-blonde twenty-something. He pours our wine with the languid air of displaced ambition; a rancorous cherub.

'Thanks, Robert. This is Louise.'

'Hi, Louise. Nice to meet you.' He doesn't sound convinced.

I like gay bars. I find them relaxing. I sense that Malcolm has loosened up too because he starts to talk about his new show. He tells me all about the bizarre hang-ups some of his dancers have about their bodies.

It's fascinating talking to Malcolm. Like a woman, he is

actually interested in the way people think, what motivates them. Gossip, I suppose you could say.

Next we go to a restaurant. This is cool as well. Pale green walls and natural wood everywhere. The chairs clatter and it's full of people our sort of age, talking greedily and swilling back the wine. We have another bottle with our fish. They only do fish. Mine comes with the head on which makes me think of Kevin and I laugh. I tell Malcolm a little about him, not breaking confidence, just chatting.

'Sounds like a completely straight guy.'

'He is.'

'Well, maybe that's his problem.'

'No, I don't think so. I've already considered that but I think it's more complicated. I think it's to do with trusting people. He has very high expectations.'

'And you said you bumped into him in Camden? That must have been weird for him.'

'Yes. He was with his girlfriend. She seemed nice. A bit dull, maybe, but then he would play safe. He's incredibly defensive.'

'But he came to see you. That's taking a risk, isn't it?'

'Well, you'd think so. Except that he seems to see our sessions as a kind of testing ground. He keeps everything close to his chest, as though he wants me to take the risk. To jump in.'

'Well, why don't you then? Shock him.'

'Yes. I might well do that, you know. One of these days. That was delicious.'

'Good. By the way, you look fabulous tonight. I've never been out with a woman who looked rich and tasteful at the same time.'

'Oh thanks. They're usually one or the other, are they?'

'They're not usually anything. I'm very choosy, you know.'

'And the men?'

'Man.'

'Just the one?'

'Yes.' Malcolm goes quiet and pours himself the last drop of wine.

'Sorry. I didn't mean . . .'

'It's okay. I'm a bit sentimental about him.'

'That's okay. I understand.'

'He died.'

'Oh God. I'm sorry.'

'No, I'm sorry. It was a long time ago and the relationship was over anyway.'

'And you haven't been with a man since?'

'No.'

Malcolm pays the bill and we stroll back into the crowded streets of Soho. Gangs of drinkers are herded onto the pavement outside the clutch of sweaty pubs that dominate this corner. It's loud and lively. Everyone shares a sense of new energy, of release. It's the weather. And I feel strangely uplifted too. Maybe it was the conversation. For all my credentials I'd rather be going out with a man who sticks to women.

By this time nobody appears to give a fuck what Malcolm is wearing. There are some pretty strange outfits on show, but I haven't noticed any other men in skirts. I put my arm round his waist and he looks down at me.

He puts his hands on my face and bends down to kiss me. A deep, tender kiss. I like people who kiss in public. It's life-affirming.

'Wha-hey!' A cheer goes up behind us and we pull apart to see a gaggle of lads raising their glasses to us. Malcolm grins at them.

'Get stuck in, mate,' a deep voice shouts.

'Nice totty,' another one growls. I look at Malcolm. I'm not sure whether they mean him or me. He kisses me again and the cheer is echoed. So, maybe people aren't as backward as I sometimes think.

We walk hand in hand up the middle of the road, smiling at each other mutely.

'My club?' Malcolm asks when we get to a junction.

'Sounds a bit posh.'

'You'll like it.'

'Sure. Whatever you say.'

We climb down some steps towards a dungeon on one of those narrow roads that leads north to Oxford Street. Inside it is dim and smoky. I can make out various couples strewn around each other on diverse sofas and tables. Malcolm leads me through a homely, carpeted room where some arty types are talking frenziedly, and up a small windy staircase.

There is a nook with a tiny bar, bottles of expensive wine ranged across its counter, but nobody serving. He picks up a bottle and two glasses, guides me up another crooked stairway and ducks into an oddly shaped room which also has a crooked floor and a sagging ceiling. But it has the most authentically delapidated leather sofa I have ever seen. I immediately sink into it. Malcolm gets a corkscrew and ashtray from a cupboard as if this were his home and joins me. There is a small puff of air as he lands on the cushion next to mine and I roll towards him.

'Fancy a fuck?' I slur at him.

'I was hoping you'd ask me that,' he says and pulls down my boobtube leaving my tits exposed. I laugh my dirty laugh. He looks at me.

'You do my head in, you know, you crazy bitch.'

'Just get on with it,' I lie back and smile while he covers one nipple and then the other with his mouth and his hands. It's like bathing in sex. Levitation by pure lust.

I close my eyes and imagine my whole being has become liquid. I can no longer tell where the sofa ends and my body begins. I lose track of where his hands are, and where I am . . .

'Louise, Louise. Wake up. Come on, darling. Wake up.'

I open my eyes. I seem to have slipped halfway onto the floor and my knickers are disappearing up my bum. I've no idea how long I've been laid out like this; like some abandoned old whore. But Malcolm is still there, smoking.

'Hello.'

'Uh?' I grunt.

'You fell asleep,' he is smiling at me.

'Oh God, I'm sorry. Look at me,' I start to adjust myself. 'How could you leave me like this? What if someone had come in?'

'Darling, I've been charging admission fees for the last half hour.'

'Oh no, I must look like a drunken old tart.'

'Don't worry about it. You're pissed and stoned, that's all.'

'Really?' He nods and kisses me. 'Oh God, what a wreck. I'm sorry. How terrible.'

'Come on, girl. Get with it. We've got the rest of the night yet.'

'What do you mean?'

'I mean, we're going on to another club.'

'Oh right.' I pull my clothes together and look at him in the half-light. 'Malcolm, you're not going anywhere like that.' His cock is practically bursting out of his skirt. I slide down onto my knees and pull the wrapover skirt apart.

'Oh Louise . . . mmm . . .'

This would look fairly odd to a passing stranger. A man standing with his back to the door in a long skirt and high-heeled boots with a smart-looking blonde going down on him. But it's the kind of place where you figure nobody would give a toss. I didn't know gentlemen's clubs were like this. It's a first for me, anyway.

After we've both cleaned up in the antique loos we meet at the entrance. Malcolm gives me a glass of water.

'Ready to dance?'

'Mmm hmm.'

'Want to have a good time?'

'Mmm hmm.'

'Good. Take this.' He slips a small tablet into my hand.

'What is it?'

'It'll keep you awake.'

'Okay.'

We get in a taxi and hurtle across London. I've got no idea what the time is, but most of the crowds have dispersed and there are only a few chastened souls wandering the streets, searching for a nightbus.

I've never been to this club before, either. It's a huge warehouse with three separate rooms and each one is thumping out a different kind of music. Several people seem to know Malcolm. He introduces me a few times and we all grin and laugh and cling on to each other like old pals. And when I get the urge to dance, we take over the floor and Malcolm throws himself into it, all the time grinning at me and laughing. I do the same. It's a brilliant night.

By the time people start drifting off into the morning I am completely shagged out, but happy. I've found a kind of energy I've never felt before and even though my body is tired I still feel alert. I kiss a few people goodbye. God knows who they are, but they all kiss me back and we flop into a black cab.

Back at my flat I make a tray of tea and toast and take it through to the sitting room. I switch on the telly. Sport or news. That's all. I wonder when the cartoons start. Do they still have cartoons on a Sunday morning?

'Louise. I need to sleep.'

'Oh no. I don't feel tired at all.'

'That's because you've led a sheltered life.'

'Well you go to bed then, old man. I'll come up later.'

'But Louise, it's nearly daylight outside. You need to get some kip.'

'No I don't. I need to eat and watch some telly. I'm fine. I had a fucking amazing night. You're absolutely wicked. And now I feel too good to go to bed.'

'Okay. But don't say I didn't warn you. You're going to feel like a dog that's been run over in about four hours.'

'Okay, fine. I'll let you know.'

I don't feel like eating, so I channel hop through an assortment of really distressing remedial television and then reluctantly decide to go to bed. It's getting light outside. I pull back the sitting room curtains and throw the window open, breathing in a lungful of early morning tonic. As I blink and squint out at the road, something seems to move down by the gate. Probably next door's cat. Or I'm not in control of my sensory apparatus. Definitely time to sleep.

When Malcolm wakes me I look at the clock. It's half past one in the afternoon. He's wearing his skirt again. He says he has to go. He's got a bloody rehearsal and has to go home to change first because he says they'd lose all respect for him if he turned up in a skirt.

I don't want him to go. I feel completely dreadful, like my head has been in a vice all night. My body doesn't want to move and I feel terribly scared that if he goes he won't come back.

'What did I do? Did I do something awful?'

'You were wonderful,' he bends down and kisses my neck.

Malcolm's got this satin negligee with fake fur round the collar and cuffs which he likes to wear round the house. I pull it on and follow him down the stairs so that I can kiss him on the doorstep.

As Malcolm walks off towards the tube I wonder if it's possible – if I can really allow myself to fall in love with this man so soon after Malcolm. I watch him turn the corner. In the midday sun his skirt looks like a beachwrap. I think I love him already.

There is some litter lying by the gate so I tiptoe down the steps in my bare feet and pick it up. I look at the scraps of paper. An empty envelope, torn into four pieces. When I fit them together I can read the name scrawled across the front: LOUISE.

sixteen

SUNDAY EVENING I've perked up a bit. It was only the drugs, whatever they were. Malcolm says that when you're feeling tired or really low you should fondle your earlobes. Honestly, he says you should get each one between finger and thumb and give it a good rub and twiddle. He says it releases energy and makes you feel hot.

He also says that if you're in the shower you should find the vertebra just below the small of your back and rub it, quite hard. Then work your way right down to the base of the spine. He says this is the centre of energy and that most energy is sexual. I agree. It certainly does the trick for me

I'm round at Nicole's flat. She called me up to go through some preparation for Tuesday's prison group.

I love Nicole's flat. There is nothing on the walls and nothing to fiddle with. Huge plate glass windows slide open onto her tiny balcony which overhangs the manicured private garden. She lives on the eighth floor and the view from this room is of trees and green contours. But if you stand on the balcony and turn slowly through 180 degrees, you can see all of London's multiple personalities unfurl until you sense the muted throb of the city – pressed layers of dank geometry that is essential London, ancient and modern. These familiar features are what make us urbanites feel connected and real.

The smell of fresh coffee pervades every room and Nicole joins me with a tray of crockery and pastries. She gets outrageous cakes from a Polish delicatessen down the hill and seems to eat them all day.

'So, how's life? You seem pretty animated lately.'

'Ah, it's love, you see.'

'What does he do, by the way?'

'He's a choreographer-cum-teacher-cum-artistic genius.'

'Do you mean he's a bum, or does he have some talent?'

'I don't know yet,' I laugh. Malcolm is definitely not a bum although he's poor.

'And what have you done with your old, discarded Malcolm?'

'Hey, less of the sympathy. It was him who dumped me, remember, and I have waved my last goodbye to him. Well, for a few months, anyway.'

'Very good.'

Nicole pours the coffee. For some reason I feel slightly uneasy with her today. She's being too polite.

She hands me an envelope and says,

'Read it.' I suddenly remember the envelope I found by the gate this afternoon. But this is different writing, addressed to the clinic. Inside the envelope is a single sheet of A4 paper, covered in childish print. An anonymous letter, all about me.

There's a list of the things this person would like to do – teach me a lesson, basically. And then it goes on about what a bad mother I am, what a bad counsellor I am and how I am good for nothing except punishment. It's utterly mad, ranting, vicious nonsense. Some of the sentences are unfinished and quite a bit of it makes no grammatical sense at all. But the meaning is clear enough.

Nicole watches me read it. I try to laugh, but I can't. She asks me gently if I think Malcolm could have written it.

'I'm only asking because it's unusual to see your name. This may be someone who knows you.'

'No.'

'Well, I just wondered. With you splitting up, you know.'

'No, Nicole. Why would he? It was him who finished it anyway.'

'I know. But people can do strange things when they're upset. Maybe the sight of you with another man after all these years is just too painful for him.'

'But this is so pathetic,' I scan the letter again in disbelief.

'Darling, it happens all the time. I don't show them to you unless they're specifically about you. I don't see why you should be bothered by them. It's quite predictable, really. You know what people think of us.'

'Yes. That we're "the whore's abortion".' I quote randomly from the page that is still clenched in my shaking hand. 'Jesus, Nicole. I had no idea. Are they all like this?'

'I'll show you if you like.'

Nicole disappears and comes back with an orderly file from which she hands me a sheaf of paper. All anonymous letters, about twenty of them, catalogued in clear plastic with labels on.

'Why do you keep them?'

'I don't know, really. I should dismiss them, but somehow they interest me. Like most perversions, there is something terribly human about them. Somebody is pleading, begging for understanding. And also, if anything did ever happen to one of us they might be useful.'

I read a few of them. My face burns. I happen to have picked out a particular group of them which are about Nicole.

'Are they all like this? So personal?' I don't know quite how to say it, but some of the letters have picked on Nicole's own obsession – her weight. I know they must have hurt her.

'Oh no,' Nicole laughed. 'It's only because I've categorised them by their content. I try to find the key, the particular fear that has made them do it. You see this one, the one that mentions you, is about power. The power of sex. You see how it accuses you, and then "whore" and "abortion". It is about your sexuality as power. That's why I thought it might be someone who knows you, rather than a client. It is definitely someone who feels scorned.'

She notices me frowning, trying to work it out.

'Don't worry about it, darling. It's pointless. These people are innocuous. That's the whole point. Anonymity is the only way they can express their feelings of anger, of rejection. It really is nothing to worry about.'

'Still, it would be nice to know for sure who it is.'

'Well, think about it this week. You may be able to work it out. If it's not Malcolm, it's someone who wants your attention. They'll want to make sure you've got the letter so they might even drop a hint; goad you into confronting them.'

'Have you ever confronted anyone?'

'It's never happened like that. I have realised in a few cases who it is, but as soon as they think you know, they disappear. It's their weakness that makes them do it in the first place, you see. They can't actually face you.'

I nod. They just skulk around when they think you're not looking, I think to myself. How cowardly.

seventeen

AT THE PRISON ON Tuesday, Ted, Richard the doctor and two others from last time are waiting for us. I'm quite nervous. This will be my first time talking with them. Nicole has a word with the warden and James is allowed back into the session. He's creepy. He makes me think of the anonymous letters.

I read out one of the victim statements we found in our research which makes me shake a little. When I read them to myself at Nicole's flat they didn't seem so awful, but sitting here in this cold, bare room reading aloud to five convicted sex offenders, woman-haters, makes me feel vulnerable.

I don't look up until I've finished. There is a silence. The men sit with their heads bowed, all except Richard who is looking at me. I look back.

'It's very unfortunate,' he says, eventually.

'I'd kill him,' one of the others says. Then there is silence again.

'Ted, how do you feel about this woman's story?' Nicole asks him. He looks up and then he says something really surprising.

'I don't know, man. What would you think? You never hear his side of the story. I mean she could've provoked him. Maybe she was taunting him. Maybe she asked for it. They were married for a long time. How do you know what she did to him?'

'That's a good point, Ted. How do we know? We've only got her story to go on.'

'I don't think any woman would ask to be treated like that,' says Richard.

'You don't know, man, you don't know what she did to humiliate him. You don't know what was going through his head.'

'But even if we did know what was going through his head, Ted, we know the victims were not asking for it. We've admitted that before. Maybe we should try and work out what was going through her head, hmm? Maybe she did tease him, maybe she did provoke him, but do you really believe she wanted that?'

'I don't know. I just think you should give both sides of the story, you know?'

By the end of the session, when I've read out a couple more testimonies and we've discussed them, we've had tears from Ted and one other. Nicole thinks this is good. I am not so sure. I'm not sure whether getting them to identify with the victim won't make them feel even more isolated and misunderstood than they do already. And that self-pity could turn them back towards random aggression.

We have a long discussion about it in the pub afterwards. I decide to do the training course Nicole has mentioned to me. I need to tackle my own prejudice.

eighteen **18**

THURSDAY, 4.50PM. The weather is completely gorgeous again. It's like me at the moment – doesn't know what it's doing. One day it's miserable and overcast, the next it's brilliant crisp sunshine.

Today I feel vibrant. Malcolm and I had a cosy evening drinking wine and talking about ourselves. He's pulled a muscle in his back so I had to be very gentle with him. He's got the most amazing collection of underpants I've ever seen. Last night's were black gauze with garter straps at the sides, just like women's knickers, but with this soft, rubbery material for the pouch. Very nice to touch.

I'm on the phone talking to Henry. He says he can't afford to come in. Petra's gone off to New Zealand and he's worried that she won't come back. I try to reassure him, but he's got himself into quite a state about it. He's terrified of losing her. I ask him if he's had any auditions. He really needs to find something to focus on. But it turns out to be the wrong thing to say. He thinks he will never work again. Poor Henry.

I've just put the phone down when Kevin comes in. I turn to smile at him from my perch on the arm of the sofa.

'Stay where you are,' he says, his back pressed against the door. Then he puts his fingers to his lips. He tiptoes over to the bookcase and looks behind it, then he gets down on his knees and looks underneath the sofa and the armchairs, then creeps over to the window and with his back against the wall, peers round the curtain to look outside.

'Okay. All clear,' he sighs out with his hand on his chest.

'What are you doing?' I ask, bemused.

'Just checking, Louise.'

'For what?'

'Spies. You never know who might be listening. I don't want everyone knowing our private business.'

'Kevin, you know our sessions are completely confidential, don't you?'

'Oh yes, of course. Of course they are. You mustn't mind about me, Louise. Just trying to amuse you.'

I shake my head, smiling.

'You see, you're smiling. You can't help it, can you? Go on, Louise, admit it. I brighten up your week, don't I?' I am still smiling. 'You see, you see. I know how to make you smile.' And he plops down on to the sofa, triumphantly.

'Kevin, I thought maybe we could talk a bit more about your parents, your family. Carrying on from last week.'

'Oh no, Louise, you didn't believe all that, did you?'

'Shouldn't I?'

'Oh no,' he claps his hand to his forehead in a cartoon gesture. 'I'm sorry. I must have judged you wrong. I thought you were clever. I thought you'd have seen through that, Louise, you of all people. I didn't think you were that gullible.'

'Wasn't it true?'

'Well, what do you think?'

'I don't know. Why don't you tell me?'

'Ah, well, the thing is, Louise. I can't stay this week. Busy, you know. I just popped in to say hello, really. Don't want to let you down. I know you look forward to me coming,' he winks.

I do actually, but I wouldn't let him know that.

'You don't have to, Kevin. You just need to phone up and cancel if you can't come.'

'Oh, I wouldn't do that, Louise. I've made a commitment to come. I wouldn't go back on my word. Anyway, I've got to go. You take care of yourself till next week,' he touches my arm in a friendly way.

I want to say something to him; something reassuring. But as he leaves he pretends to walk into the doorframe and totters about as if he's going to fall over. Stupid sod. But it's true, he does brighten up my Thursdays.

Malcolm comes over for the whole weekend this time. No rehearsal space. It's only been four weeks but I think we're going steady. Something about Malcolm makes it okay to do things in front of him that I would never have done with a man before. It seems that we have all the time in the world – we don't have to fuck every minute we're together like Malcolm and I did.

We paint each other's toenails on Friday night and eat ice cream in bed. It's a bit like having a girlfriend staying over. Except that he likes to watch me masturbate. I've never done that with a girlfriend.

Gerard is staying over as well and Malcolm shows him and Timmy some kickboxing moves which is enough to turn them into an adoring fanclub. I promise to take them to the show when it opens.

On Sunday we leave the boys at home and go off to the heath to meet some friends of Malcolm's who are having a picnic. They're mostly dancers so I'm surprised by how sloppy and average they look. One of the women, Claire, seems to want to latch on to me and talk about Malcolm. She says it's good to see him with someone who understands him.

'What do you mean?'

'Well, because you're a sex therapist. I mean you must have come across people like Malcolm before. You can understand why he's so mixed up about his identity.'

'Is he?' I didn't realise he'd told all his colleagues what I do. It's a pain.

'Well, obviously. I mean otherwise why does he feel the need to put his feminine side on display all the time? It's classic. It's all to do with his mother.'

'Is it?' It has never occurred to me to ask Malcolm about his parents. He seems perfectly well-adjusted to me.

'Maybe he doesn't want to tell you about it because of your job. But when I was going out with him he talked about his mother all the time.'

'Did he?'

'Oh yes. He never stopped going on about her. That's why I finished with him in the end. I couldn't compete. He's a lovely man, though. Don't get me wrong. I'm sure with you to help him he'll be able to sort through it all. I mean we've all got our baggage, haven't we?'

'Yes. Yes, I suppose we have. I'm just going to get some more food.' I have to get away from her because she makes me want to punch her in the face. I determine never to ask Malcolm about his mother, however curious I might be feeling. I don't want to know about his past. I like him the way he is.

'So, what did you think of them?' he asks me as we walk home.

'I liked them.'

'So do I socially, when I don't have to kick their arses into gear. Paul is really talented and Chrissy, but the rest of them are lazy bastards. Did you talk to Paul?'

'A little, yes. I could tell he was your favourite.'

'What do you mean?'

'Oh, something about the way you kept looking at each other.'

'I don't fancy him if that's what you mean.'

'Don't you?'

'No. Well, not anymore, anyway. Not since I met you.' He gives me a big bearhug. 'You should see him dance. Everyone falls in love with him. It's the curse of talent. He's got no sex drive at all, poor lamb. He spends his life completely mystified by other people. He lives to dance. And that's what makes him so good to work with. And to watch. You wait, you're going to love this show.'

'Good. I'm looking forward to it.'

'Who else did you talk to?'

'Well, I got cornered by that awful woman, Claire.'

'Oh, yes. Claire and I had a thing once. It was a disaster. You should never try to have relationships with your dancers. It's professional suicide.'

'I didn't like her.'

'No. I can understand that. She's not bad really, but she's got a lot of problems, Claire.'

I smile to myself. That's all right then.

Malcolm's got his negligee on.

'God, why are you wearing Mum's new dressing gown? You look like a right poof,' Timmy says to him, executing a shadow kick to his stomach and spinning round.

As he raises his leg again Malcolm grabs his ankle, not completely in jest.

'When you've got that right, then you can call me a poof, okay.'

'Urgh. You've got nail varnish on,' Timmy counters bravely while struggling to balance on one leg.

'Don't you like it?'

'It's girlie.'

'That's right. And I know some girls who'd have you on the floor if you tried to kick them like that,' he lets go of Timmy's leg. He's not really a bully.

'So what?'

'Well, I mean that they like to be butch sometimes. But they're still girls. I like to be girlie sometimes. What's wrong with that?'

'Nothing,' Timmy pauses, thinking. 'But don't people laugh at you?'

'So what? I don't care.'

'Well, I wouldn't go round with nail varnish on.'

'Yes, but you can't do this, either.' Malcolm puts one arm round the small of Timmy's back and spins him up off the floor and over his shoulder. 'Now call me a poof.'

'Okay, okay. Put me down.'

'No.' Malcolm holds him there with one arm. Timmy starts giggling.

'Put me down,' he screams.

'What do you think, shall I put him down, Louise?'

'Do what you like with him.'

'Okay,' he spins Timmy back down to the floor.

'Poof,' he yells and races upstairs. Malcolm is grinning.

'He's a macho little bastard, isn't he?' I say, quite proudly. 'He must get it from his father.'

'He's fine. He'll get used to me in a year or so,' Malcolm walks behind my chair and starts massaging my shoulders with his strong fingers, pressing hard into little knotted muscles I didn't know I had.

We are having a relationship. A steady one. We both know it. Neither of us has said 'I love you' yet, but we both know it's true. Already I can't imagine my life without him. It's timing. It's the right time.

nineteen

SUMMER HAS DEFINITELY arrived. People are showing bare flesh in the street and smiling at one another. I've got a few new clients filling up my diary where old ones have dropped out. Mr Daniels has gone, thank God. He's moved to a City firm and won't be able to make it up here anymore. He should be able to find a grateful, undiscriminating tart in EC1 to give his spare cash to. Good luck to her.

There's been another anonymous letter. Nicole hands it to me on Thursday morning. It's the same writing, but the content is different this time. It goes on about what he'd like to do to me again, then the second half of the letter is apologetic. He says he wants to get close to me, to look after me. It's a bit spooky. I prefer the obscene fantasies.

I'm no closer to working out who it is. Self-preservation reasons that it's one of the prison inmates – they can't actually get to me, so they write letters. I don't want to take it too seriously, but on the other hand I can't help feeling unsettled.

At five o'clock on the dot Kevin comes in. He's looking tanned and fit. The perfect man to chase your blues away. He grins at me, his wicked blue eyes glinting, and rubs his hands together.

'Louise, I've made a decision,' he announces from the doorway. 'I'm going to tell you everything. I've decided it's the only way.'

'Good.'

'Only, I don't want to tell Dr Padremans,' he whispers, looking over his shoulder. 'Not yet. I don't feel comfortable with her. Is that okay?'

'Yes, Kevin. Come and sit down.'

'No, I'll just stand if you don't mind.'

He looks around as if confirming that we're alone. I'm sitting on the sofa with my notebook.

'I'd like to put some music on. Do you mind?'

'Go ahead.'

He chooses some ambient jazz. He seems to spend a while just listening, psyching himself up, or calming himself down. I wait.

'The truth is, Louise, I'm not a very nice person,' he pauses and walks over to the window, looking out in that slightly paranoid fashion.

'Would you mind if I asked you to put your notebook down? I'd feel more relaxed.'

I put it on the table.

'And would you look away. It might put me off if you look at me.'

'Okay, Kevin. When you're ready.' I fix my eyes on the floor. The music is unsettling. Inappropriate somehow.

'I have done some things in my life which I'm ashamed of. And I've never told anyone about them. I think that's why I can't get close to anyone. I mean, I know I've got lots of mates. Everyone at church thinks I'm a great guy. My family think I'm a great guy. Good old reliable Kevin. But I'm not.'

I look up for a moment. Kevin is standing with his back to me, looking out of the window. He is tense. If this is another performance, it's his best yet.

'I want to tell you this, Louise, because I think you'll understand. I think I can trust you. I know you've been waiting a long time, but I had to be sure. You can understand that, can't you?' He spins round to look at me. I meet his eyes.

'Yes, of course.'

'The thing is, Louise. I'm looking for an answer . . .' he stops. I don't respond.

'You didn't say anything.'

'What do you want me to say?'

'I thought you would have the answer, Louise.'

'To what?'

'The mystery, of course.'

I look up and wait for him to explain. Kevin shrugs and smiles at me for a while, sadly. Then he suddenly starts flailing his arms around and jerking his body.

'What does this remind you of?' I'm completely taken aback. Kevin is doing a kind of psychedelic dance routine. He is rotating his whole head in time to the music and rolling his eyes as though he were having some kind of fit. My first impression is that he's really lost it this time – he is a nutter. Then I want to laugh. But he continues arsing around just a minute too long and I actually feel myself getting quite cross. Like I do sometimes with Timmy – an irrational, intolerant reaction.

'Go on, Louise. Who am I?'

'I don't know, Kevin,' I'm biting my lip. He stops and throws his arms out in despair.

'I'm not very good at dancing,' Kevin sits next to me, panting, gives me a petulant look and then breaks out into laughter. I laugh too. It doesn't dissipate the tension, though.

He straightens his face just as suddenly as he laughed and says, 'That was an impression of me. Don't you see, Louise? I'm like someone who's taken drugs. They think they're having a great time, they think they're letting go of all their inhibitions, that everyone likes them. But really they're stupid, blind, ignorant. That's me.'

Kevin takes my hand and stares into space for a moment.

'I'm looking for the answer, Louise. And you know what it is.'

'Do I?'

'Yes. The meaning of life, Louise.' He squeezes my hand

quite hard. 'What is the meaning of your life, Louise? Oh fair Louise, pray tell me.'

I frown at him, but he is serious.

'Well, that depends.'

'On what?'

'On what I'm doing, where I am, who I'm with. There is no single purpose, Kevin. At the moment for instance, I want to be able to understand what you're going through. To help you.'

'To help me? You think you can help me? To find my meaning of life?'

'Well, only you can do that, Kevin,' I say, giving him my best conciliatory smile.

'Oh great. That's the eternal cop out for you lot, isn't it? You let us talk and make pratts of ourselves and then you say, "only you can help yourself". Let me tell you something about me, Louise. Let me tell you something that will make you realise why I am the last person able to help myself.' He moves away, facing the wall and fidgets with his hands.

'I'm not like other men, Louise. But you don't mind that, do you? You don't judge people by appearances. You're unusual too. It's a gift. You make people feel normal, acceptable, even when they're outcasts. You're a good person. That's why I want to tell you the truth about me.'

I shift my bum on the sofa. I suddenly had a flash of the last anonymous letter, the childish scrawl and that phrase; 'You're a good person'.

Kevin goes over to the bookshelves and picks out a book. I don't look. I can hear him leafing through. Then he starts reading.

' "When I was a child, my speech, my outlook, and my thoughts were all childish. When I grew up, I had finished with childish things. Now we see only puzzling reflections in a mirror, but then we shall see face to face." '

He comes over to the sofa and sits next to me with his head in his hands.

'Do you know what that means, Louise? What it's saying is that even when we think we know, we don't. We don't know anything. We will never understand the mystery of life. Do you believe in resurrection?'

I hesitate.

'I don't know.'

'We never know, Louise. We can never be sure . . . of anything. But we have to put our faith in God. Do you understand?'

'I don't know, Kevin.'

'That's okay. You will. When I was a child, Louise, I was really happy. My life was simple. Being a child, I thought it always would be. You don't expect things to change. But everything changes, your whole identity. I was christened Elvis.'

I look up. He catches my eye and grins.

'You see, you didn't believe me, did you? I told you that was my name the first time I came to see you. But I knew you wouldn't believe me. I don't look like an Elvis, do I? I look like a typical paddy. A builder. Kevin. It's a good Irish name. Elvis Presley died when I was seventeen anyway. My mum cried. Elvis Kevin Mary Ryan. That's my name.'

I grin back at him. He's very charming when he's talking honestly. I wonder why he doesn't do it more often. He's interesting. It would be good to get to know him properly.

'Bet you didn't know a boy could be called Mary.'

'No, I didn't.'

'You see, there is always something to learn, even from an old dinosaur like me. Anyway, Elvis was my mum's idea. She was a bit of a raver when she was young,' Kevin throws his head back and laughs at this. Really laughs. He seems more manly, more adult than he has ever seemed before. I realise how much I've been taken in by his childish mucking about, his alter ego. He suddenly seems in control, open and comfortable with himself. A breakthrough.

'So, I'm going to tell you the story of Elvis. Are you sitting comfortably?' he winks at me. Then he looks down and becomes more serious. 'I'm sorry, Louise, no more joking. I want to tell you this. It's about me. It's about my life. I want you to understand.'

'That's good, Kevin. I will listen.'

'Oh, I know you will. I don't have any doubts about you, Louise. I feel I know you now. It's me. I . . . I don't know if I can do this.'

I wait.

'Okay. I'll tell you about Elvis. Ready?'

'Yes, I'm ready,' I smile encouragement at him. He looks away and gets up again.

'He was born in County Wicklow, on the east coast of Ireland. It was a large family. Catholic and Republican. So, Elvis knew about violence and he knew about love. Love of God, love of country and love of family. That is what they taught him. He was a good son. He always helped his mother with the smaller children, like a girl,' Kevin pauses and looks at me.

'We all have a masculine side and a feminine side, Louise. You know about that, don't you?'

'Yes. I'm sure that's right.'

He turns away again and starts pacing, clenching and unclenching his fists.

'Do you mind me talking like this?' he looks at me. I smile and shake my head.

'Elvis was courteous and obedient to his parents and the priest. The English television did not seduce him like it had wooed the others. He was a simple child. He loved the grass, the rain, the soft talking of religious men. Perhaps he would become a monk or a priest; a poet. He was not interested in girls. Even when his younger brothers were already trying out their carnal instincts he did not succumb. He was pure.'

I sneak a look at Kevin. He is standing by the bookcase, his head tilted up towards the light, his eyes closed. His speech is like a script, something that he's memorised, but his voice is clear, not inhibited at all. I wonder how long he has been practising.

'The boy Elvis was small. His puberty was late. At the age of fifteen his voice had been artificially lowered through secret rigorous training, inspired by the choirmaster in Dublin who chose him out of all the village yokels for special treatment.'

I am still looking at Kevin, somewhat mesmerised. He squints at me and smiles.

'I put that bit in for you. Because you said I was a peasant.' I laugh.

'Oh, but I don't want you to think there was anything, you know, weird going on. No. It wasn't like that. I know you read in the papers about weakness and perversions in the Catholic church these days, but this was untainted, Louise. They were innocent times. You do believe me?' I nod. Kevin closes his eyes again and folds his arms.

'When Elvis was a teenager, he couldn't help noticing in the changing rooms after rugby practice, or in the bath at home, that the other boys had grown these . . . um . . . well, these hairy sacs between their legs where all he had were . . .' Kevin clears his throat. 'I'm sorry, Louise. This is very difficult for me to say. I was underdeveloped. A late starter. I think it's important. All the other boys had larger . . . um . . . they used to parade them, sometimes when they were . . . well . . . erect. But Elvis was too shy. He had no hair on his body and the dreams that woke him up frightened him. He just wanted it to stay what it had always been – a winkle.' Kevin opens his eyes and looks at me. 'It's all right, Louise, you can laugh if you want.'

'I don't feel like laughing, Kevin.'

'Oh, okay,' he nods and makes a mock-serious face. 'I'll carry on then.'

'And the other boys had shadows on their top lips. But he was as clean, as girlish as his sisters,' he stops and scratches his head.

'Do you think that somewhere there is a woman who could love a man who was effeminate, Louise? Could you, for instance?'

'I . . . I don't know, Kevin. I'm sure someone could . . . of course.'

'Don't worry. Only teasing,' he takes a deep breath.

'Elvis braved it out by being the joker. They never caught him. They never got a good look even in the showers. He was faster, cleverer, funnier than them. He thought he was lucky. He didn't understand the changes the other boys were going through and he didn't want it to happen to him. He knew he was different. He believed it was Jesus. Singling him out,' Kevin smiles at me.

'Honestly, Louise. I know you might find this hard to believe, but in those days, in a small place like that in the country, you didn't have all these gadgets to distract you,' Kevin waves his arm round the room.

'I mean all these computer games and new sports. I don't know how parents keep up with all the equipment they are expected to buy. Everyone has to have the right gear. But we just had a ball and plenty of fields. And we felt close to God. You would too, Louise. In Wicklow Hills. You should come over one day,' Kevin squats by my feet and looks up at me soulfully. I nod, trying to look non-commital. He snorts and abruptly leaps up.

'When Elvis was seventeen, disaster struck. Within the space of one week it seemed, his testicles dropped, his voice truly broke, he grew hair and shot up three inches.

'The boy became a man. Overnight. And he was scared.' Kevin is pacing again, getting into his stride; his animation filling the room.

'Not of the responsibility. Not of losing his innocence, nor of being inadequate in the face of new physical expectation. But scared that God had cast him out, that Jesus had deserted him. He must have done something bad and would now be relegated to a normal life like all the others. When what he wanted above all was to be special. To be chosen. Singular. He could play at being one of the gang. He was accepted as one of the gang.

They loved him. He was so funny, so smart. He was everyone's favourite mascot.

'But his secret, lonesome life as Jesus's friend . . . his destiny . . .' Kevin pauses and clears his throat.

'He resolved to be celibate. To regain God's confidence. He didn't know what he had done. Well, he suspected it was his daydreaming about Imogen Ryan, the doctor's daughter,' here Kevin pauses again and sneaks a look at me. I catch his eye and we both smile. Then he starts declaiming again.

'But whatever it was he would do it no more. He would make himself perfect. He would continue his pact with Jesus as if nothing had happened, to maintain his purity, his distinction. Because he wanted his secret mission. No matter how long it took, Jesus would eventually send him a sign. A sign that he had been forgiven and that things were back on course,' Kevin fixes my eyes as if he expects me to confirm this. Then he turns his back to me again and continues talking to an imaginary audience.

'So, at the age of seventeen Elvis had resolved to live his life according to a plan. Not many teenagers do this. They are mostly so haphazard; trusting that nothing will be taken away from them, that stability will go on for ever. But Elvis knew from a young age that once you have made a mistake everything is lost. Everything you have believed in, that has secured you, held you solid and comforted against the great adult tempest of change.

'And knowing this, he learned an early lesson. The lesson that struggle, abstention and tightness – keeping yourself close – is beautiful in itself. The joy of knowing that you can do anything they can do, but that inside you are unaffected by the carnival of relationships, of worldly dreams and shattered expectations. That is beauty. And it is strength.'

Kevin's passion makes my nerves tingle. All this time he's been entertaining me, making me laugh, making me like him. And now it's as though I knew this other side of him all the time. It was always lurking under the surface. This devotion.

'Sure, Elvis was one of the boys. He was a good fly half, a good swimmer, he played pool reasonably and he loved fishing. He was not bad at school but he knew that wasn't really important. To be a good person, that is important, Louise.

'He had stopped singing in the choir and he knew he was just marking time. There seemed little to keep him in this tiny village. So when his two schoolmates decided to go to England for work he agreed to go along. Why not? His family duty as the eldest son could be safely passed over to Mary, the oldest girl. In any case, he knew things about his family that the others didn't know. He had felt for some time that they were a bad influence. They distracted him from his real work, the work of finding his true family,' Kevin lets out a vocal sigh a bit like a moan.

'His mother had been ill. Well, not ill exactly. She became pregnant during Elvis's last year in Ireland. But she was getting old, she had given birth to seven children already. She rejected the unborn from the first moment,' Kevin's voice gets really quiet at this point in his speech. Not exactly a whisper but as though he's afraid someone else might hear. He appears to be calm and carries on talking with a wide open expression on his face, looking just past me.

'Only Elvis saw this, only Elvis sat up at night, wide awake with a kind of wakefulness that is more alert, more sensitive to threat than daytime consciousness. Only Elvis heard their conversations, the endless arguing, the bitterness. His father's first true baby. And his mother, who had never really loved her husband, who had lived a lie for twenty odd years, did not want it.' He pauses and wanders round the room.

'Only Elvis heard. And only Elvis did not care. He did not want the child born either. He didn't want to see himself and his siblings made into changelings by this new being. He hoped and prayed for some misfortune to befall his mother. He willed the baby to die inside her. He prayed to Jesus to do this thing, to take the unborn soul straight to heaven where it belonged, where it would remain forever innocent. And he wouldn't mind if his mother died as well. She could be saved then.

'A few weeks went by. It was difficult to keep his knowledge to himself, but Elvis had been training himself. He would be the most private person on earth if Jesus required it. He did not even tell the priest. Father Ignatius didn't need to know everything that occurs between a man and God. God sees all.

'The others noticed that their mother was not well. She was often sick and bad-tempered. Their father appeared nervous, unlike himself. He started going to the pub, leaving his wife alone with her sins.

'Then, one day, when Elvis came home from school his youngest sisters were there before him, playing jacks on the doorstep. "Ma's upstairs in bed. The doctor's here. She's been bleeding. Do you think she'll die?" His prayers had been answered. Elvis went to his room and shut the door. He prayed hard, thanking Jesus, thanking Mary and all the saints for their good work. Now he knew, now he understood. He would do God's bidding from that moment until he entered the Holy Kingdom and nobody, but nobody would distract him from this purpose,' Kevin sighs and shivers, letting go of the memory.

'The miscarriage left the family scarred. Only Elvis and his next brother down, Michael, had an inkling of what had taken place. But everyone was different from that day. Their father turned into a brooding old man – a failure. Their mother decided she would be a martyr. She still cried alone at night, tears for her lost baby. But Elvis knew they were tears only for herself. Because she never wanted the child, because she was a sinner, because God did not deem her worthy of being carried off by the angels to that glorious rebirth. She was infected. Elvis kept his distance. She deserved her unhappiness.

'So, the decision to go to England was easy. He wondered why he didn't think of it himself. Everyone goes. Either to England or America. There is nothing in Ireland for them.

'In Liverpool there was no work. Even for three strong, willing workhorses. They stayed a week and then headed off to London. And Elvis has never been back, never contacted his family, he left them behind and now he has a new life.'

Kevin stops. The music finished ages ago. There is a long silence. I don't know what to say. He comes over to me and strokes my cheek like a lover.

'Hey, I didn't mean to upset you, Louise.' I smile at him.

'It's a very moving story, Kevin.' How much of it is true, I wonder.

'Shall I go now?'

'No. We should talk.'

He sits down next to me, his eyes gleaming with exhilaration.

'Kevin, I want you to think about what you've just told me. I want you to think about it and tell me whether it really is the truth of what happened. Whether you believe that that is what happened.'

Kevin frowns and moves his body away from me.

'I'm disappointed in you, Louise. I really am. You just don't get it, do you? Or are you playing games with me? Of course it's the truth. I wouldn't ever tell you a lie, Louise. I wouldn't ever lie to you. Don't you understand? I'm different from other men, Louise. I'm different. I wouldn't ever lie to you.'

'Okay, okay, Kevin. I believe you. I do. I just wanted to be sure. Because, you see, if what you just told me is true, if you truly believe that you were the cause of your mother's miscarriage then I think we need to talk about this.'

He turns towards me, pleadingly.

'In fact, Kevin . . . I think it's very important. I think it may give us the key to why you find it so difficult to trust people, to be intimate with them . . . to trust yourself. Kevin, do you see? Do you understand?'

Kevin nods, looking overcome.

'The first thing we have to talk about, Kevin, is your relationship with your mother before this happened. Before she had the miscarriage. You say you had a happy childhood. I want you to tell me more about it. Do you think you can do that?'

He nods again, but he doesn't speak.

'Why don't you start by describing your parents' house to me, Kevin? Just close your eyes and go back in time to when you were about seven or eight. What can you remember? Where was your bedroom? Did you share a bedroom? What colour were the walls?'

There is a long pause. Then he speaks, 'We didn't have duvets. We had cotton sheets and blankets . . .' he stops.

'That's good. What else?'

'I can't . . . I can't remember. It's no good, Louise, I can't remember. But I think you're right. I think now that I've got it off my chest, now that I've told you, I think it'll be all right. I just needed to be able to trust you. I know now . . .' He is moving towards the door.

'Kevin, don't go yet. Kevin . . .' But he is not listening to me.

'I think I know what it is now, Louise. I knew you'd know the answer. Look, we'll talk again next time, okay? God bless.'

'Kevin . . .' Kevin has gone.

I wait, half-expecting a knock on the door, hoping he will compose himself and come back in. But there is nobody out there. I open the door and Sheila smiles at me.

'He was in a bit of a hurry. What did you do? Get your tits out?' she cackles.

'Ha bloody ha. If he calls, anytime – I don't care – I want you to get me. Day or night, okay?'

'Okay sweetheart. Don't blame you. He's a bit of all right,' Sheila is chewing. I pinch one of her toffee eclairs and sit on her desk.

'Oh Sheila, I don't know. He's so fucked up, poor guy. But he will not let me help him.'

'He's besotted with you. Anyone can see that. He doesn't want to make a fool of himself. I'd have him, even if he is fucked up.'

'Were you listening?'

'No. But maybe I should.'

'Yeah, maybe. I think somebody should anyway.'

I go back to my office and think. I need to talk to Nicole. How can Kevin believe all this? He's got me under some kind of spell with his stories and his fooling around. I find myself listening to his voice in my head, telling me over and over, 'You're a good person, Louise'.

My intercom buzzes. It's Nicole.

'Have you got any more appointments?'

'No. I'm done.'

'Okay, I'll come down.'

'I think I know who wrote the letters,' I say when she comes in.

'Oh yes?'

'Kevin.'

'What, the cute Irish guy?'

'Yep.'

'Yeah, I suppose it would figure. He's terribly defensive, isn't he? Did he tell you?'

'No. But he repeated that phrase "you're a good person", you know, just like the letter.'

'Is that all?'

'No. He just delivered a half hour speech which I think was complete fantasy from beginning to end, but designed to make me think he's nuts.'

'Why does he want to make you think he's nuts?'

'Because he wants to get my attention; get me involved.'

'Has he ever asked you out?'

'Sort of. He kept on about me going fishing with him once. But it's always ambiguous. I never actually know when to take him seriously and when he's just taking the piss. He wants to be understood, listened to, but he doesn't want to take any risks. So he makes everything a joke.'

'Has he ever tried to get you to touch him? I mean, there are far more straightforward ways for him to get what he wants.'

'No. But that's just it. He wouldn't want it on those terms, at the clinic.'

'So, he's got a crush on you?'

'Yes. I think so. And there's another thing. Someone's been following me.'

'Have they?'

'Yes. It's happened a couple of times now, on the way home from here. I thought I was just going mad, but now I realise who it was. I recognised him, you see.'

'What, like that time you bumped into him in Camden?'

'Jesus, of course. That was ages ago . . .'

'Well, if he has been following you . . . Let's assume you're right. We need to do something about it.'

'Like what?'

'Well, call the police in, of course.'

'No. No. We can't call the police on Kevin, just because he fancies me.'

'Louise, if he is following you about, checking up on you, writing letters about how you need a good thrashing . . .'

'No. Leave it with me for a bit, Nicole. Let me think about it. It might not be him. I could be wrong.'

It's just not possible. Not Kevin. Kevin's like a mate. I mean, I look forward to his sessions, he makes my week worthwhile. He's a good person, really.

twenty

THERE IS NOBODY following me home tonight. Nobody at all. I phone Malcolm when I get in, but he's not there. Why not? I need him. Timmy is here, though.

'Timmy, come here. I want to ask you something.'

'What?'

'How would you feel if Malcolm moved in with us?'

'When?'

'Well, I don't know. Soon.'

'What for?'

'Well, for good. I mean, do you think it would be nice? Would you like it, having him around?'

'Are you going to get married?'

'No, I don't think so.'

Timmy leans against the oven and flicks through a computer magazine.

'Well?'

'Can we get one of these?'

'What?'

'One of these?' He shows me a paper shredder advertised in the magazine.

'Timmy. I am not made of money. Anyway, what would you want one for?'

'For secret documents.'

'What secret documents?'

'Mine. Or yours.'

I pause, confounded.

'Timmy. Just wait a minute. I asked you how you would feel about Malcolm moving in here. How did we get on to secret documents?'

'Dad's got one. He says it's . . . um . . . yeah, "imperative for anyone who works from home". So that other people don't read about what you're doing.'

'Timmy. Never mind what Daddy said. What about what I just said?'

'What?'

'About Malcolm. Would you mind if he moved in here?'

'Where would Dad stay?'

'I don't know. He stayed at Martin and Lisa's last time he was over.'

'Okay.'

'Okay what?'

'Okay, he can move in. When are we going to see his ballet?'

'It's not a ballet,' I pause and hold my face in my hands for a moment. 'Timmy, this is a serious question. We've never had anyone else living with us properly. I mean, Daddy was always away on trips. This would mean a big change. He'd be here every morning and every evening.'

'Yes, I know. I'm not stupid, Mum. If you want him to live with you, that's fine. But I think you should get a shredder. Just in case. I mean, I don't read your stuff because I know it's private. But he might not realise. Okay?'

I laugh, more in defeat than comprehension.

'Okay.'

I open a bottle of wine. It's a habit. I try Malcolm again. He's still out so I call Emma and ask her to come over.

Half an hour later, I'm telling Emma all about Kevin. It's easier to talk to her than to Nicole. For one thing, Emma's not my boss. But she's also more open. More willing to accept that there are grey areas. For instance; when I tell her that Kevin is extremely fanciable, and that when Malcolm stormed out because of the flowers Kevin had sent me I felt a kind of self-satisfaction – that I was flattered – Emma is okay about it. I can admit it to Emma. Because actually, Kevin is someone Malcolm was right to get jealous over. I enjoy his company. I like the way he looks at me and talks to me. It's different from all my other clients. In fact, it's different from anyone I've ever met.

There's a terrible taboo among therapists which forbids you talking like this. It's not done. You're in a position of power and your clients have to able to trust you. They're supposed to be defenceless. But often it's not like that at all. They can be manipulative as well and sometimes you find you've only got your intuition to guide you; all your training counts for nothing. You're human – you can be vulnerable too.

Emma understands that. But she is also sensible enough to suggest that I should have talked to someone sooner and that I should either stop treating him, or get someone to supervise our sessions. I tell her about Nicole's reaction to my suspicions, about calling the police. Emma thinks it's stupid. She thinks I've invented the man following me – he's a manifestation of the subconscious – a symptom of my guilt. She's probably right. And she thinks the anonymous letters might be from Mr Daniels – far more likely to be from someone who is out of reach than someone who is still having therapy. I love Emma. She's much more serious than people give her credit for.

We're getting pissed, discussing the least savoury of our clients' misfunctions, when the phone rings. Timmy is upstairs doing his homework, so I grab the phone. It's Malcolm. He's had a bad day at rehearsals and wants to come round.

'Okay, my final word on Kevin and then I promise not to mention him in front of your man.'

'What is it?'

'I think you should go for it. Ask him straight out if he wants to have sex. You've got to deal with it sooner or later. He's building you up into this perfect woman in his head, he thinks he's falling in love with you. And you're not helping by just letting him go on and on about his family and God knows what. It would sort things out once and for all. You'd give him what he needs and he'd get what he's paying for. You'd both get this obsessive thing out of your systems,' Emma stops to gulp some more wine. 'Am I right?'

'Yes, Emma, you're right.'

'Right then, that's settled. Now, where's this man of yours?'

'He's on his way. I'm thinking of asking him to move in with us.'

'My God. That's a bit sudden.'

'I know. Well, it's partly because I've been getting paranoid. You know, about my imaginary stalker. But maybe that's why I invented him. Maybe I was just looking for an excuse to ask.'

'Why do you need an excuse?'

'Oh, because . . . because . . . well, you know what I'm like. I have to be self-sufficient. I have to believe that I'm perfectly happy on my own.'

'Well, you were. And now you want more. Okay? There's nothing wrong with that.'

'Really?'

'Really. You should ask him to move in because you want to. Because you want to be with him. Not because you want to feel protected. Since when have you needed a man to stand up for you?'

'Yeah, you're right. I should, shouldn't I?'

'Definitely. Well, let me vet him first and then if I give you the okay, go for it.'

'What would I do without you?'

'Tie yourself in impossible knots probably.'

The doorbell goes.

'Here, open the next bottle, would you, darling. Malcolm's got a bit of catching up to do.'

I let him in. He looks dreadful. He's wearing tracksuit bottoms and a stained T-shirt and carrying a large holdall.

'I'm sorry. I know I must look a sight. Let me just sneak up to the bathroom. I'll have a quick shower, brush some make-up on and you won't know me.'

'Of course, if you want to. We were just getting pissed.'

'Sounds heavenly. Oh, here,' he pulls a bottle out of his bag and hands it to me.

'Champagne? What's the occasion?'

'I'll tell you later. It needs to go in the fridge.'

'I did tell you Emma's staying the night, didn't I?'

'Well, she can join in. That is, unless you want me to go.'

'No, darling. I want you to stay. I want you to tell me all about your horrible day and see if Emma and I can cheer you up.'

'Good. That's just what I need,' he kisses me lightly on the cheek.

'Is that all I get?'

'Wait, darling. I've got to clean up. I've been working all day and I stink like a baboon's armpit. You wouldn't like it.'

When Malcolm's showered, shaved, changed and put his mascara on we settle down to a good gossip. He's only two weeks away from opening night so he's pretty stressed out and he says he's had to dance all day because Paul has injured himself. Then he says a weird thing.

'Do you know, I could swear someone was following me from the tube tonight. I was so desperate to get here, I didn't really think about it, but when I was in the shower I remembered what you'd said the other day about someone giving you the jitters. There was a bloke just standing at the top of the stairs when I came out of the station. He looked as though he was waiting for someone, but then, every time I had to cross the road, I looked round and he was there. Always at a distance. He came right down your road.'

'What did he look like?'

'Oh, pretty average. Short hair, quite stocky, sunglasses . . .'

Emma raises her eyebrows at me and I nod, subtly. I don't want to talk about Kevin in front of Malcolm.

'Hold on, you two . . .' I'd forgotten he is still sober. 'Is someone hanging around? Has someone been pestering you, Louise?'

'I don't know. Maybe.' Emma gives me a warning look.

'Well that's it,' Malcolm gets up and walks over to the window. 'Yes. He's there. Come and have a look.'

Emma and I charge across to him and look out. Sure enough there is a man standing across the road looking up at the house. It's too dark to see his features properly but I'm trying to remember where I've seen that posture before, when all of a sudden Emma, who never wears a bra, pulls at the buttons of her blouse and flashes her tits at him. The man looks around for a second or two and then heads off, hands in pockets, scurrying away.

'Did you recognise him?'

'I don't know, I'm pissed as a fart,' she says helpfully. Malcolm is sitting on the sofa, rocking backwards and forwards, laughing.

'Emma, you're a star. That was priceless.'

Emma doesn't laugh, though. She is doing up her buttons.

'I don't like it, Louise. I don't like it one little bit.'

I'm trying to place him. It definitely wasn't Kevin. But there was something awfully familiar about the size and shape of him, the body movements. I light a cigarette as Malcolm leaves the room, still chuckling. He comes back in with the bottle of champagne.

'Louise, I was going to ask you about this anyway, but now I'm doubly sure. I think it's time we stopped pissing around. I think I should move in here with you and Tim. I want us to live together. What do you say?'

'What?'

'You heard.'

'Well, I don't know . . .'

'Don't listen to her, Malcolm. She's been wanting to ask you herself for ages. She told me earlier.'

'Have you? Do you mean it, Louise?'

'Well, yes, I suppose . . .' I frown at him and then at Emma. My brain isn't working fast enough for this.

'Well, that's settled,' Malcolm pops the cork and pours three glasses of champagne. Timmy appears in the doorway looking sleepy.

'What time is it?'

'Why aren't you in bed?'

'I was. You woke me up. What's all the noise?' Malcolm disappears and gets another glass for Timmy.

'We're celebrating, darling. Malcolm's going to move in.'

'Great. Are you moving in too?' he says to Emma.

'Not today, Tim. Although it's not a bad idea.'

'To us,' Malcolm raises his glass. We all drink a toast and then I escort Timmy back up to bed. I lie next to him for a while.

Some time later, Malcolm shakes me.

'Darling, it's gone midnight. Emma's gone to bed. We didn't know what had happened to you,' he whispers.

'Oh. Oh, I must have fallen asleep. Sorry.'

'Sshh. Tim's asleep.'

'Oh yes,' I kiss Timmy on the cheek and tuck his sheet in.

'I love you, baby.'

'I love you too.'

'Bed?'

'Mmmm.' Malcolm puts one arm behind my legs and picks me up like I'm a small child.

'What have you and Emma been talking about?'

'Oh, you know, work . . . you.'

'Oh . . .' I cling on to his neck as he negotiates the bedroom door. Then Malcolm suddenly spins me round and round until I'm giddy.

'Oh, Louise . . .' he says, laughing.

'Put me down,' I gasp. 'What did you do that for?'

'Because I'm happy. Oh, you don't mind do you, Louise? Fair Louise, don't be cross.'

'I'm not cross, you just surprised me, that's all,' I stare at him, a little disorientated. He just reminded me of Kevin. Bloody Kevin – why does he have to appear at a moment like this? It makes me petulant.

'Do you really want to move in here?' I ask in an unfriendly voice.

'Yes.'

'But what about Timmy? He's always around, you know. Won't you get pissed off with him?'

'I adore Tim.'

'But what about all your stuff? I mean there's no room.'

'I haven't got much stuff.'

'And I can be really moody, you know. I hate other people's mess and I like to be on my own a lot of the time.'

'So do I,' he leads me to the bed and starts taking my clothes off. 'But I like being with you more.'

'Do you?'

'Yes. You are like a beautiful, wonderful sister, you know?'

'So are you,' I answer, woozily.

'Thank you,' he laughs. 'I love you, Louise.'

'Me too.'

'Well that's that then. It'll be fine. You'll see.'

'Will it? I don't know . . .' I sigh and fall into the pillow, trying to puzzle things out. I've got to do something about Kevin. That's why he plagues me, because I haven't got anywhere with him yet. It is time to stop pussyfooting around.

twenty-one
21

THE NEXT TIME I SEE Kevin the heat is debilitating. I feel slothful and dirty. But he is looking gorgeous in a crumpled linen suit. I think again how attractive he is and why on earth does he keep coming to see me. He won't open up, he will not tell me anything. His dramatic stories, just like his funny ones, are designed to keep me out; to distract me. I'm worried that if I ask him straight out about the letters, or whether he's been following me, I'm going to lose him. But something has to happen. He says he will tell me everything when the time is right. I'll just have to make it the right time.

'Do you believe me?' he asks. He is always asking me questions. One after the other. It bugs me.

'To be honest, I don't know whether to believe anything you tell me, Kevin.'

'Uh oh,' he goes.

'What?'

'Louise is in a bad mood. I can tell.' He does this mock concerned look and puts on a babying voice to ask me what's up. He chucks me under the chin then asks, 'Why do you think I come to see you, Louise?'

'That's a very good question, Kevin. Most people come to see me because they need some help. With a problem.'

'And you help them.' A statement.

'I try.' Another.

'And what do you think my problem is, Louise?'

'Do you feel that you have a problem?'

'Yes. Yes, I do.'

'Do you want to talk about it?'

'No. Not right now.'

'Do you find it helpful, at all? Coming to see me?'

'Sometimes. And sometimes I think it's the other way round.'

'What do you mean?'

'I mean, Louise,' he pauses to take my hand, holding it and looking right into my eyes. 'That sometimes I think it is you who has the problem.'

'We all have problems, Kevin.'

'Yes, but you're like me, aren't you? You don't like to talk about it.'

'If I thought it might help . . . If I felt that I couldn't resolve a problem on my own, then I would talk to someone about it. Talking can sometimes lead you to a different understanding, Kevin. I find that, don't you?'

'I don't know. You see, I can't talk to anyone about my problem.'

'Why is that?'

'Well, let's put it this way, Louise. When you do your talking, when you talk to "someone" – who is that someone?'

I don't answer. I keep on looking at him. He still has my hand.

'Who do you talk to, Louise, when you have a problem?' he smiles and squeezes my hand. 'Who?'

'Well, I suppose, first of all I would talk to a friend, someone I trusted.'

'And what if you didn't have any friends?'

'Is that how you feel, Kevin, that you don't have any friends you can talk to?'

'You know I don't. That's not the point, Louise. The point is who would you talk to, if you were me?'

'Well, that would depend on what my problem was. There are all sorts of people who can help with things. But they would need to know what the problem is.'

'Clever,' he lets go of my hand. 'But it won't work,' he gets up and paces a little. Then he sits on the bed. He bounces slightly, as if he were testing the mattress, then swings his legs up and lies back. We are both silent for a moment.

I tell myself to take the plunge. Kevin is lying still on the bed. He is asking for it.

'Would you like me to put some music on?'

'Yes, whatever,' he says, dreamily.

I choose some soft Mozart – a clarinet concerto – and move round the bookcase pressing a small button which will alert Sheila to monitor the session.

We do this for security and legal purposes. If there's any trouble Sheila has a phone number which can instantly bring a private security firm crashing in. She will also now be taping our conversation through a discreet microphone system Nicole built in a few years ago when a client tried to take us to court for indecent assault.

My sessions don't often get this serious (I am more conventional than the others), but I find these moments both electrifying and calming. Like treading round a sleeping tiger. I find myself breathing more deeply and swallowing, but my head is clear and focused.

Kevin is motionless on the bed, his eyes closed. The music is heavenly. I pick up the remote control and move quietly to the chair nearest the bed.

'What are you thinking of?' I ask, in my most soothing voice.

'You,' he says, without hesitating. I wait. He will say more. This is a routine we have both been expecting for some time.

'I'm thinking of you, naked,' he goes on, slowly. This is more like it.

'Louise, naked, is like gold. She is soft. She shines. And she longs to be molten, to meld with the moment. She wants fire,' he stops for a moment and shifts on the bed, then pushes each shoe off with the other foot.

He doesn't speak again for some time, so I try a quiet prompt.

'Where is she?'

'Louise is sitting on the floor. She has one leg stretched out and the other bent under it. Her hands are on the floor behind her shoulders and her head is tipped back. She's looking up at something.'

'What is she looking at?'

'Her neck is long and thin,' he ignores my question. 'Tanned. But her breasts are round and pale. They sway and swell almost imperceptibly with her breathing . . . like the moon on water. Her stomach is soft. Gently curving,' Kevin pauses for a moment and breathes in slowly. He exhales, clearing his throat. I am taut as a live wire.

'She stretches out her arm so that I can see sharp ribs through her golden skin and the finest aura of tiny blond hairs. It lifts my spirit. Her presence is like light. She murmurs desire from her waiting lips. Louise is ripe with sensual energy.'

He pauses again.

'And where are you, Kevin?'

'She is looking up at me. I am a man. I am standing over her. My body is pumping with anticipation, my heart aches for her beauty. She is powerful. And so am I.'

He stops again. I'm not sure quite how far to push this. It is the most amazing breakthrough. As if Kevin just decided that today is the day and came in with one purpose in mind. I try to think what Nicole would do. There is no doubt about it. With this one she would go the whole way.

I wait in silence for a moment and take a long breath in, keeping very still.

'Have you talked like this to anyone before?'

'Oh yes,' Kevin reaches down and touches his left thigh, leaving his hand to rest there.

'It's very sexy, Kevin,' I say this as slowly and unthreateningly as is humanly possible. He still has not opened his eyes.

'I feel sexy, too,' he says. 'I always feel sexy when I'm near Louise. She turns me on.'

'Would you like to turn her on?'

'Yes. Yes, very much.'

'What would you like to do to her?'

I am still very calm, in fact I'm enjoying this. It feels private and thrilling. Not like a job at all.

Kevin is not speaking. He is breathing in and out very deeply and emanating little sighs in time to the music.

'Louise is here,' I say. 'She likes being with you.'

'Does she love me?' he says.

'Do you want her to?'

'I don't know. She intrigues me. But I'd like to know. I'd like to know how she feels.'

'How do you think she's feeling right now?'

'I think she's getting turned on. I think Louise wants to have sex.'

'With you?'

'I don't know.'

'What do you want, Kevin?'

'I want to feel her – her pussy, her lips. I want to feel how wet she is. I want her to give herself up to me, to melt in my arms. To become one with me.'

I wait. Kevin's voice, and the music . . . his stillness, the soft, perpetual thudding of the fan and the heat, the things he's saying . . . actually make me feel horny. I force myself to think of Sheila outside the door, listening.

'What else, Kevin? What would you like to do now?'

'I'd like to make her orgasm. I could be Louise's lover. I would protect her. I would do anything . . . anything she asked. I would breathe on her neck and hold my hand against her, where she guides me – pressing down in that special place – the way she likes it. I could make her quiver. I'd like to suck her breasts, her hard nipples and kiss her stomach. I want to make her happy. I want Louise to be mine.'

'Do you want to have sex with her, Kevin?'

'No.'

I wait again. This is his fantasy.

But Kevin doesn't speak.

'Why not?' I ask eventually.

'I want to make love,' he says, softly, a slight crack in his voice. I look at him, wondering if he might be about to cry. That wouldn't be unusual at this stage.

'I love Louise. I want to make love to her.'

I draw up some reserve of professional detachment and move to the side of the bed. I lean close into Kevin's ear and whisper, 'Louise is here. Would you like to make love to her now?'

'Yes,' he says.

I momentarily consider a hundred things – should I turn the lights down; should I wear the surgical gloves we were all issued with for dealing with Aids sufferers; where exactly are the condoms; is the music about to end; should I set up the video as well as Sheila's audiotape; tell him to keep his eyes closed; keep my eyes closed; keep one foot on the floor; give him a sextoy instead; or kiss him.

'Are you ready, Kevin?' I say instead, playing for time.

'Yes,' I can barely hear him.

'Do you want Louise to take her clothes off?'

Silence. His hand unconsciously strokes his thigh again. I notice the swelling contour of his penis, pushing out the creases of his linen trousers.

'Do you want Louise to touch you, Kevin?'

'Would you kiss me first?' he says.

He doesn't say, "I want her to kiss me", or "Would she kiss me", he says "You". And I am so fucking arrogant – thinking I'm in control – that I don't even care that he has suddenly switched to the second person. I don't protect him. I deserve to be struck off for this.

'If you want me to,' I say, like a sacrificial lamb.

'Yes,' he says. I lean in and kiss him lightly on the lips, then move away quite quickly.

Kevin keeps his eyes closed, but a half smile forms across his face.

'Come here,' he says. I come close again.

'Let me feel you,' he says. I put out a hand and touch his chest.

'Let me feel your cunt,' he says, forcefully. I take a sharp breath in, slowly take his hand and press it between my legs. I have a fairly short skirt, so Kevin's hand is right against my knickers. But his fingers are limp. He doesn't seem to want to feel me. I keep his hand there, with my hand over it. I really am turned on. I can feel an ache spreading like hot wax across my pelvic muscles and I know he must be able to sense the moistness seeping into my knickers where I am pressing his hand . . . firmly now.

The music has finished. We stay still and quiet for a few seconds, Kevin's fingers not quite engaging with anything so that my desire is becoming treacherous. And then suddenly, so suddenly I gasp with shock, he pulls his hand out of mine, sits up and opens his eyes.

'Only joking,' he says, grinning brightly. Then he jumps off the bed, slips his shoes on and heads for the door. He turns back.

'You would do that for me?' he asks.

I don't say anything. Kevin tuts three times, rolls his eyes and leaves. I am so surprised I just sit for a while, thinking about nothing. Shivering in the fan's warm breeze.

I come to as the buzzer goes. It is Sheila.

'Everything all right in there?'

'Yes, Sheila. Everything's fine.' I wander over to the table and turn the radio on for distraction. You stupid, stupid cow. What have you gone and done?

I don't talk to anyone. I just pack up my stuff and head to the pub for a gallon of beer or gin or whatever.

George greets me.

'Hello, blondie. Cheer up.' I smile faintly. 'Oh dear, that boss of yours been giving you a hard time, has she? Tell you what, I wouldn't want to cross swords with her.'

He pours me a pint and brings it over to the table.

'You meeting someone then?'

'No. Thanks, George.'

'Oh, it's just someone was in asking for you earlier.'

'Were they?'

'Yes. Could be your lucky day. Ask Carol – she spoke to him.'

Him? I can only think of Kevin.

'Carol, Carol,' George grabs her arm as she wafts by collecting glasses. 'Who was that bloke asking for Lou?'

'Oh yeah. He asked if I knew a blond woman who worked in an office round here.'

'I thought he said her name – Louise.'

'No. I never said that,' she rolls her eyes in contempt.

'Oh well. Sorry mate,' George heaves himself back behind the bar leaving me alone to ponder Kevin.

After about ten minutes Nicole walks in and comes over to my table.

'Thought I'd find you in here.'

'I've been kind of expecting you, too. Beer or wine?'

When I come back with the drinks she has lit one of my cigarettes.

'Nicole, what are you doing?'

'Smoking.'

'But why?'

'Why not? You do.'

'Yes, well, you don't want to use that as an excuse. You'll find yourself in all sorts of dumb situations.'

'Like this afternoon?'

'Ha ha.'

I sit down and light a fag myself. I can imagine what's coming next. Nicole takes a long drag on her cigarette and blows out two perfect smoke rings.

'That's pretty cool,' I say. I've never been able to do them.

'Anything you can do, I can do better,' Nicole is smiling at me.

'Oh yeah?'

'Yes.'

'I've never heard of you offering yourself wantonly to a client . . . only to get a slap in the face.'

'Did he slap you?'

'No. I was speaking metaphorically.'

'Well if you're going to be like that . . .' Nicole stubs out the cigarette.

'Picture this,' she leans across the table, an intense look on her face. 'There's a family of cats; the domesticated type. One kitten has been injured in a fight. It limps home to mummy. Mummy sniffs around to make sure the coast is clear and then nuzzles the kitten. It rolls over, showing its bloody wound. She puts out her tongue and gently starts to lick away the debris, but the wound is so raw, so painful that the cat squawks and jumps up. It hobbles off to a far corner to rest, its little heart pumping vibrations through its tender body.' She sticks her bottom lip out like a manipulative child.

I laugh.

'Very cute image, Nicole. What happens to the mother? Does she lose her job?'

'No,' Nicole tuts at me. 'She's got the rest of her litter to worry about. So, one little runt wants to sulk in a corner and suffer all by itself, so what? She leaves it.'

'Thanks,' I say. It doesn't sound quite right, this stoic little story, but at least she tried.

'I'm not trying to make you feel better, Louise. It was a pretty dumb thing to do. But what matters now is what we are going to do next. You know he's got a thing about you, we think he's been following you, we think he's been writing the letters. What do we do now? Now that you have let him get that close. Do you think he's got what he wanted?'

'No. Oh, I don't know.' I feel sulky.

'You know, Louise. When I first went into therapy, many years ago, I had a problem with my work. I thought that something must have happened in my past, something that my conscious mind was blocking off. Something that meant I couldn't deal with the kind of pressure I was under. So, my therapist – he was a hypnotist – tried some regression therapy. And it worked very well. I did find out about my past. And I found out that there was nothing there that really explained the way I felt. Nothing at all. I just couldn't stand the thought of failing. That's all it was. I tried to avoid it, to look everywhere except at myself for the answer. I suppose because I had always been very ambitious. My whole family were ambitious and I didn't want to appear weak; to be seen to be failing.'

'So what did you do?'

'Well, when I realised that, my therapist basically told me to move on – to sort my life out. And I did. I quit. By that time I felt that I had moved on so far that I didn't want to put myself through any more stress. I hated sales anyway. I wanted to get on with my life and put it behind me. That's when I started re-training as a therapist myself.'

'Right. Well, you know that it was you, helping me through those first years with Timmy that made me go back to college as well. And I thought it was the right thing to do. I thought I could help people. But maybe I don't want to. Maybe it's all about me . . . really.'

'It's often the case,' she pauses and puts her hand on my arm. 'Stop beating yourself up. We all make mistakes, Louise.'

'But I don't even know what I've done to him. I'm angry with myself for being so stupid. But I haven't thought about Kevin. He needs help.'

'Don't we all? You can't always win, Louise. Sometimes you are not the right person. If he wants to be helped, he'll try again.'

'And maybe he won't.'

'That's right. Maybe he won't.'

Nicole takes a long drink of her beer, wipes her mouth and leans back, relaxed – her face a picture of receptiveness.

I know I'm going to have to talk to her eventually, but I don't want to. I groan.

'Oh Nicole. I know what I've been doing.'

'Take your time.'

'The trouble is, I really like this client. I mean, you've met him. He's funny and clever and very good-looking. And he's also naughty. I mean, he mucks me about, he has no respect for what we do. And I saw him as a challenge ... but then the letters, the feeling that I was being followed ... I didn't want to believe it was Malcolm, but even more I didn't want to think it could be Kevin. I like him.'

'Sounds reasonable.'

'Yes, but I've been so confused. First Malcolm walked out on us, then I met this Malcolm. And now I'm falling in love with him. Oh I don't know. This sounds corny, but when you're in love, it's like being in love with everyone. The whole universe seems to be made of loving, lovable people. I could shag anybody right now. I know that sounds disloyal and everything. But that's what it does to me. I feel invulnerable, turned on, positive about everything. And most of all, I suppose I feel valued. And that's something I want everyone else to feel. I want to give everyone a bit of what I've got. God, I sound like Mother Theresa or something. Does any of this make sense?'

'Of course it does, darling. We all know that feeling. It's called euphoria.'

'Yes. Yes, that's what it is. So, there I am with Kevin. And he started it. He came in and just lay on the bed and started talking about having sex with me. And I lost it. Just lost my professional distance and allowed myself to respond. But it's strange. Because it's exactly what I was going to suggest to him anyway. It's almost as if he knew what was going through my mind. He's often like that. He senses my moods, he challenges me about things that have happened to me.'

'And what do you think now? Did he send the letters? Has he been following you? Maybe he just wanted to see how far he could go with you.'

'Why couldn't the letters be from Daniels? Why do you think it's Kevin?'

Nicole sighs. She motions to George and asks him for a whisky.

'Darling, did Mr Daniels ever show the slightest reluctance to tell you what his problem was and what he wanted from you?'

'No.'

'In fact, isn't he the one that pissed you off so much because you felt he just wanted servicing and never intended to get therapy at all?'

'Yes.'

'So, what makes you think he would have to resort to anonymous letters? Hmmm? When he was always more than willing to tell you his fantasies and get you to perform them for him.'

'I don't know. But Emma said . . .'

'Oh, Emma. What does Emma know? Emma has never had a client like Kevin. In fact, Emma's never had a client like Daniels. Emma deals mostly in physical disability, you know that.'

'Yes. I suppose so. So, what the fuck am I supposed to do now? Do you want to call the police?'

'No. I've thought about it and I've listened to the tape from this afternoon. I don't think Kevin's dangerous. It would be completely out of character,' she swills her whisky around in the glass, thoughtfully. 'But he is persistent.'

'So how do we get rid of him?'

'I don't know, Louise. You're in the position now where he gets to call the next shot. Of course, from his point of view you've been in that position all along. The difference now is that you know. And that may change things for him, too. It's just possible that he'll give up.'

'Poor Kevin.'

'Poor Louise,' she raises her glass to me.

Nicole and I get very pissed that night, talking about loads of personal stuff. She wants to understand everything about everyone, does Nicole. Maybe that's why she's always been on her own.

twenty-two

I WAKE AT ABOUT FOUR in the morning trying to work out what might have happened if Kevin had responded to me. I can no longer pretend that this was a straightforward relationship with a client. I've never actually had full-blown intercourse with any of my men (Nicole and Emma do it, but I do mainly handjobs). So why did I choose Kevin?

The answer has to be because I actually feel something for him. And I've managed, quite spectacularly to deny this to myself right the way through six months of so-called therapy. When I think about it, it's obvious that all Kevin has ever done is flirt with me. And I've encouraged him.

I groan inwardly and roll over, pulling the sheet away from my body which is sticky with the night's sweat. Malcolm is sleeping soundly, unaware of my infidelity. But it is him I love. Kevin's just been a projection of that. I've allowed Kevin to get away with his behaviour because somehow I've made him part and parcel of my new relationship.

I can't stay in bed. I get up and grab Malcolm's negligee, tiptoe downstairs to the kitchen and put the kettle on. I light a fag and sit at the table, flicking through a leaflet advertising Malcolm's show. Inside there is a piece of paper folded up.

I gasp. A most godawful thought flashes subliminally across my brain, too fast for me to hold onto. But then I realise this is

written in the same hand as the envelope I found down by the
gate – torn up and discarded – nothing to do with the other
letters. I start reading.

Dearest Louise

*I am writing this because I am too much of a coward to tell
you face to face, or because there is never enough time, or it
never seems like the right moment, or something. But really,
I know it is because I would stumble and stutter and sound
pathetic. Believe me, Louise, however much more authentic it
might sound coming from my mouth, I could not bear it if you
didn't respond the way I want you to. So it is safer for me to
write it down.*

*We have been seeing each other for a while now. Not long, I
know, but long enough, Louise, for people like us to know what
is going on. I do not want to waste any more of my life waiting
by the phone, or feeling insecure about which shirt to wear. I
want to know. Correction. I need to know. You see, this would
have sounded dreadful coming out of my mouth. I always seem
to sound so contrived and insincere when I am with you. Which
couldn't be farther from the truth.*

*Louise, all my life, I have been waiting for someone like you.
No. For you. I have been waiting for you. There is no one like
you. How could there be? I love you.*

Louise, I LOVE YOU.

*You make me feel like a man. You make me feel that I've
found my place. I don't want to say 'I've come home' because it
sounds so corny. But at this moment, my vocabulary fails me
because that is how I feel, Louise. I want to spend the rest of
my life with you. I want you more than I can express. I love
you.*

WILL YOU MARRY ME?

I look at the letter over and over again. What on earth does he mean? Marry him? What is he thinking of?

Then I go all soppy for a few moments and daydream about a life with Malcolm; roses round the door, breadbaking and everything . . .

There is a noise outside – just a cat. But a chill runs through me and I put the note down. I don't know if I want this.

I light up again and suddenly all I want to do is speak to Malcolm – my ex-Malcolm. He knows me. He'll know what to do. I pick up Timmy's address book and scan through the long list of crossed out numbers and hotel addresses until I find the latest one. I pick up the phone and start to dial.

Then I put it down again. Why am I trying to phone my ex-boyfriend in the middle of the night to ask his advice? I take another look at the note. It's written in rough, that's obvious. It's not meant to be seen. What kind of a person rummages around, reading other people's private notes?

I wander through into the sitting room and flick through the TV channels. Nothing. I try and focus on myself. Should I marry him? Nobody's ever asked me before. How absurd and old-fashioned of him. Then again . . .

I swing my legs up onto the sofa and sip my tea. Why not? It's a fairly commonplace ideal. I curl up and pull the flimsy negligee round my neck. It smells of Malcolm. I wallow in the smell and the thought of him. And drift off.

I waste most of Friday morning fiddling around the house in a confused state. Malcolm's moving his stuff over tonight and tomorrow in the company van, so I'm trying to make space. But everywhere I look there are things – acquired paraphernalia.

I sit in the kitchen, chain-smoking. Marriage is for people in their twenties – to establish a pattern, a certainty. Or for children. It hasn't occurred to me before that Malcolm might want children. We've never talked about it. And I don't want to think about it.

His moving in is fraught. Malcolm has always lived in rented accommodation so he hasn't got much stuff – a music system, some books – but he has got an enormous trunk of clothes. We're carrying it from the van and Timmy is hovering trying to be helpful. I'm going backwards up the steps to the front door which Timmy holds open but he lets go of it a touch too early and Malcolm gets it in the face.

'Fuck!'

'Down,' I say and start to lower the trunk.

'How can I put it down when I've got a fucking door in the way?' He tries to shoulder the door back and lets one hand slip from the trunk. I drop my end and Malcolm shouts, 'For fuck's sake, Tim, get this door open.' Timmy rushes round and pulls the door open and Malcolm stands there, hands on hips, looking furious.

'Well, it's no good shouting at us. Why didn't you get one of the men to help?'

'Because they've got a fucking show to do in just over a week and I do not want to have to deal with any more injuries. All right?'

'All right, calm down. It's only a trunk.'

'Yes, well, where are we taking it?'

'I don't know. Where would you like it? In the bedroom?'

'I thought you'd sorted out some space. What the fuck have you been doing all day?'

'Oh, you know, sunbathing, drinking Pimms. What do you think? Arsehole.'

'You could put it in the study,' Timmy pipes up, helpfully. 'Dad won't be using it anymore.'

'That's a good idea, darling. Well done.'

We lug the bloody thing upstairs between us and Timmy goes ahead, clearing a space among my files and clippings which are organised in piles on the floor.

'There.'

'Fantastic, Tim. Thank God someone's got the brains round here. How about a cup of tea?'

'Okay,' Timmy runs off, all eagerness.

'Sorry. I'm sorry. I've got a lot on my mind.'

'Yes, well that doesn't mean you can just go around shouting at people like that. He's a child.'

'I know. I'm sorry. I'll apologise.'

'No, don't apologise. If we're all going to live together, we have to get used to each other's moods, you know. There's no point apologising every time you've been short-tempered. That just makes you look like a creep as well as a bully.'

'Oh. Of course, Miss Psychology. You know best,' he leaves the room and I sit with a thump on the trunk. Fuck it. That's exactly what I used to do to Malcolm. I do not want to slide into old habits.

Nobody comes back upstairs so I sit for a while, thinking. Then I open the trunk. It contains a collection of neatly folded fabrics – spangly, floaty and lacy; a dressing up box. I rifle down through the layers until I find it. A boned corset, complete with padded bust. Malcolm's alter ego.

I close the trunk swiftly and sit on it again as I hear him coming up the stairs.

'You're right,' he says simply.

'It's not going to be blissful every single second.'

'It is for me,' he leans over me, sweatily. I think momentarily of Kevin, who is never sweaty.

'I love you,' he says and we snog. It's sexy, especially the salty taste of his lips.

I push the thought of the frocks to the back of my mind. His show opens a week Tuesday so he has got a lot on his mind. It's ridiculous timing – moving in now – but he's impatient, like me.

I am also under a certain amount of pressure. Nicole has asked me to take this week's prison session on my own. It was changed from last week because of some trouble with the inmates and now she's gone off to present some of our research at a conference in Holland, so it's down to me.

I get down to work, looking through our notes and reading up on the latest stuff from America. It's weird. In some States they are just champing to get these men in the chair. They have this warped Christian morality, lumping together paedophiles, gays, rapists ... And transvestites. I'd like to go over there. I want to understand more.

I find myself talking in my head every now and then. Sometimes I am thinking about Malcolm's mute proposal. All weekend I am expecting him to say something, but he doesn't. And sometimes I think about Kevin.

23

THIS TIME AS I SWEEP across the forecourt of the prison I feel much more positive. I know my way around, the man at reception recognises me and I know more or less what to expect. I've got a plan. I'm going to ask Richard to re-tell the story of his offences but from the woman's point of view. It's something I read about in one of the more intelligible reports from the States and it seems like a worthwhile experiment. Richard is the most educated of the men and I figure he will understand what I'm asking him to do.

But Richard is not here today. He's been put back on cleaning duty because of some allegedly sarcastic remark he made to a warder. I can't imagine that any of the warders would understand a word if Richard were to be really sarcastic, but I have to accept their authority. X is not here today, either. He's in the treatment unit. I don't ask.

So, I decide to try James. At first he fidgets a bit and ignores me. But I wait. The others are yawning and re-enacting that schoolchildren's trick of making the new teacher feel like a gate-crasher at a select party. Still I wait.

Eventually, James starts to talk – quietly at first and then gathering power and momentum.

'I'm frightened. I don't know what he's going to do. I am panting. He's holding a knife. I can see the blade glittering. He puts it to my throat. I will do anything. I don't want him to hurt me. I look at his face. He hates me. I am really frightened. I want to scream but I can't because my voice has gone. I can feel the edge of the knife on my neck. I don't want him to cut me. I don't want to be cut. He tells me to get on my knees and unzip his fly. I do it. He tells me to take his cock out. I do it. He tells me to suck it. I do it . . .'

I keep looking at James. His eyes are fixed firmly on the floor and he doesn't seem excited at all, although one or two of the others are getting agitated.

'He tells me to do it faster. I can feel the knife on my scalp. He is playing with my hair. I suck his cock, faster. His cock is big and hard. I put my hand on his cock and he comes into my mouth. It tastes good. He takes the knife away from my head and puts it on the ground. Then he pulls me up by my hair and tells me to take my top off. I take my top off. He tells me to take my bra off. I take my bra off. My nipples are standing erect because of the cold. He tells me to take my skirt and tights off. I do it. I am standing in front of him in my knickers. He picks the knife up again and holds it against my knickers. I can see his cock, hard and throbbing again. He cuts through the lace. He calls me a tart because I am wearing lacy knickers. I start to cry. He tells me to shut up. He tells me he will stick the knife up my smelly cunt if I cry. I stop crying. He tells me to turn round. I turn round. He puts the blade of the knife across my back. He tells me to get down on all fours. I do it. Then he sticks his cock into my arsehole. It won't go in. His cock is too big. He pushes and pushes and I cry. Then it slides in and I scream. He pushes. Once, twice and then he pulls my hair and lifts my head up. He puts his hand over my mouth and pushes again. Then he takes his cock out and pushes me over so I am lying on my back. He tells me I am disgusting. He tells me I make him feel sick. He kneels over me and puts his cock in my mouth. He tells me to lick the shit off it. He tells me it's my own shit. He says I should eat my own shit. He pushes his cock into my mouth faster and harder and he gets hold of my tits and squeezes them and pulls them so it hurts. Then he comes on my face. The knife is on the ground. I can see it. He sees me looking and he picks it up. Then he laughs at me. He says we will all eat our own shit. He says we are made of shit. He kicks me and then he does up his flies and walks away.'

There is a long and thoughtful silence. I look at James, this man with the sadistic fantasies. This man who has carried them out on non-consenting women. One of the warders at the back of the hall is looking decidedly red-faced. I wonder what features in his fantasies.

'How do you think that woman feels now?'

James looks up at me. His face is red and tear-stained.

'Like the piece of shit that she is,' he says defiantly.

'And how do you feel?' He says nothing. But he stares at me. Stares and stares.

'James. How do you feel about what you did?'

'Like shit,' he says and his face breaks into a tortured grimace. 'Like shit, shit, shit, shit, shit . . .' he breaks down completely.

I signal to one of the warders to come over. Ted looks back as the prisoners leave the room. He knows. It's a detail – an isolated but fundamental misunderstanding – that sets James apart from those of us who keep our fantasies locked away.

I pull my chair up very close to James. I don't feel in the slightest bit scared. I feel strangely empowered.

'James?' he doesn't look up. 'James. If you want to stop feeling like shit, I think I can help you. There is medication, treatment. There is help for you. I can help you.'

James never says another word. He makes the slightest inclination of his head to signal acquiescence and half an hour later I float out of that prison like I'm tripping. I know now. I suddenly know what I want to do. No more impotents. This is what I want. I want to help these men. Because they are totally lost. Because I don't hate them.

I double lock the door when I get home and sit with Timmy for a while, watching him play on his computer. He won't show me his secret password. He reminds me of his father; so insular. Then I have to unlock the door again because poor Malcolm can't get in.

'Is this some kind of family game?' he asks when I let him through the door.

I wish he'd come clean – ask me to marry him – because I've decided to say yes.

twenty-four

THURSDAY IS CLAMMY. Kevin didn't turn up today, so I guess that's the end of it.

I miss him.

There has been another letter, though, which strengthens my belief that it never was Kevin. I think it's someone from the prison. This one talks about me being a bad mother, how I should have my children taken away from me. It doesn't say 'son', it says 'children' so it can't be anyone who knows me well.

'But how do you explain you being followed?' Nicole insists.

'Oh I don't know, maybe I imagined it.'

'But you said Malcolm thought someone followed him home too.'

'They probably did. He's very good-looking.'

'I still think you should take this seriously, Louise.'

But I don't want to think about it.

The girls take me to the pub, aware that something is unresolved. We talk about the prison work. Nicole agrees with me that we should hook up with the clinical psychiatry unit to work out our plan for a day centre.

We leave the pub some time after seven. I say goodnight to Nicole outside her flat and walk on towards home. It's early but the light is beginning to go and there is a stillness in the air. Everything seems too quiet. I turn down my habitual short cut through Highgate Village; walking fast. Sticky and heavy with alcohol.

As I turn out of the alleyway I peer back into the gloom. There is nobody there. Then all of a sudden the horizon reverberates and an electric-white spear of lightning cleaves the sky over my head. I race home and practically fall through the door, desperate for cool and safety.

'Timmy,' I call brightly. No answer.

'Timmy, are you home?' Still nothing. I pound upstairs to his bedroom but the light is off. I can hear the low rumbling of the impending storm outside. Inside there is nobody.

Gripped in panic now I rush down to the kitchen. His schoolbag is lying on the floor next to his chair and there is a note on the table. 'Gone to Gerard's for tea. Home about eight.'

I grab his little list of phone numbers from the noticeboard and phone Gerard's parents.

'Hello. Oh hello, it's Louise Chapman here, Tim's mother. May I have a word with him?'

Timmy comes on the phone sounding completely normal and a bit sulky at being disturbed.

'Darling, it's nearly eight o'clock.'

'I know. Gerard's dad is bringing me home in the car.'

'Okay. Good. See you soon then.'

When Timmy gets in he throws himself on to the sofa glumly. He sits there, staring at the TV screen waiting for the adverts to finish, and it strikes me how beautiful he is. And how I don't want strange men hanging around, strange men in our lives; spooking us. And that makes me angry.

I stand in the hall for a moment, running my fingers through my hair and thinking. It's too hot. The temperature doesn't seem to change in the evenings any more. I think we're all going to frazzle up into bad-tempered old crones before summer has even officially started. I open the front door and stand outside for a minute. The thunder seems to have packed up. I sniff the air. The rain can't be too far off.

I walk down the first few steps and look around. The light is orange-tinged and turning opaque now. There is a warm breeze and the distant whine of a motorbike.

'Louise,' somebody whispers, quite close to me.

'Who's there?' my heart stands still.

A figure steps out from a bush by the gate. It's the man. I screw up my eyes, trying to place his features. He pulls his sunglasses onto the top of his head.

'Henry?'

'Louise. I'm sorry, I just had to talk to you,' he walks towards me. I wonder if he's been drinking.

'Henry, what . . .' I start to say, but suddenly there is an enormous roll of thunder. We both look up at the sky. There is a stab of lightning. Then another, louder clap of thunder. The sky cracks again.

I look at Henry. Suddenly a familiar figure runs in through the gate, tackles him from behind and pulls him to the ground.

They struggle on the floor. I stand watching in a trance. I can't really see what's happening. They're clenched together and scuffing up a lot of dirt but nobody seems to be winning. Kevin and Henry fighting on my front steps.

There is another huge clap of thunder and enormous pellets of hail start pounding down. I step backwards up to the door, staring at the men.

'Mum,' Timmy comes to the door. 'Mum, what's happening?'

'Go inside, Timmy,' I turn round, but he is just standing there.

'Timmy go inside,' I shout.

Suddenly galvanised into action by Timmy's presence I move closer to where the men are still twisted round each other.

'Stop it. Stop it, the pair of you. Just stop it,' I am screaming.

The hail is battering at my skin and beginning to soak my clothes. There is a change of weight in the clinch, they both roll over and Kevin manages to sit astride Henry holding his face into the ground.

'Kevin. Stop it. Let go of him,' I get hold of his arm and try to pull him off. 'For fuck's sake, Kevin.'

Kevin looks up at me horror-struck and then down at Henry as if he doesn't know where he is. He stumbles up and as he turns to grab on to the gate Henry rolls over, sticks out a leg and Kevin trips, twisting his body round the prongs of the gate. He crumples to the floor.

'Kevin,' I rush over. He is doubled up in pain. 'Oh God, Kevin. Can you hear me?' He doesn't answer, but his face is contorted with agony. He looks as though he's screaming, but the hail and the thunder drown him out. Henry touches my shoulder. I look up at him. I don't know what to do. He is clutching his leg and there is blood running from his nose.

'Timmy,' I yell, as loud as I can. 'Timmy.'

He is there at the top of the stairs. He never went inside.

'Phone an ambulance!'

Kevin has stopped screaming. He is curled up and rocking from side to side.

We wait in a kind of dramatic tableau as the hail turns to heavy, warm rain. Eventually, after a lifetime, the ambulance arrives, its flashing lights a welcome focus in the steely blackness.

When Timmy and I get back inside I send him straight up to the shower. He's excitable. We talk until he falls asleep. Malcolm will be home any minute so I leave him a note and race off.

At the hospital, the first person I see is Henry, sitting in A& E, flicking through a tatty old magazine. He's got his leg up on a chair opposite and there is still dried blood on his face.

'Henry?'

'Oh Louise, thank God you came. I'm so sorry. I've messed it up, haven't I? I've ruined everything.'

'No. Don't worry about it. How's your nose?' Henry shrugs and indicates the ten or so other people sitting around in varying stages of discomfort.

'I have to say, it looks pretty bad,' I smile. It's swollen and going a sort of greenish colour round the bridge.

'It's my own fault. I don't blame him, jumping me like that. He probably thought I was a madman. Maybe I am. I'm sorry, Louise. I didn't mean to hurt your boyfriend.'

'That wasn't my boyfriend, Henry.'

'Oh. Well anyway, I didn't mean to hurt him. I can't even remember what happened exactly. I've been in a bad way.'

'What were you doing there, Henry? Have you been following me?'

'No. No,' he tries a little smile, but it's too painful. 'I wouldn't do that. I didn't mean to frighten you, Louise. I just needed to talk to you. Petra's gone. She's gone. I haven't got any money. I needed to see you.'

'Henry, why didn't you just phone? You could have gone to your GP. Oh God, Henry . . . it was you, wasn't it?'

Henry smiles, pathetically.

'It was you all along.'

'I'm sorry. I didn't know what to do. And now I've messed it all up.'

'Henry . . .' I start, but he's so hopeless. 'Henry, I know it seems like the end of the world, but you can get through this, you know. I'll help you. Just get to your doctor, for fuck's sake; he can prescribe anti-depressants; you can come and talk to me; we'll get you sorted out.'

Henry looks at me inconsolably. He really is a mess.

'Look, I'll go and see what's happening. You really ought to get that nose seen to.'

I speak to the woman at reception who says Henry will be seen next.

'Henry, I must ask you this. How did you find out where I live?'

'I'm sorry. I did follow you from the clinic once. I don't know why. I wanted to talk to you, but it seemed wrong. You look very different outside the clinic. I thought you might be cross with me.'

'So you decided to follow me instead.'

'Only because . . . I just thought . . . if I found out where you lived, I could drop a note in, or something.'

'Were you at the tube the other day, near my house?'

'Yes. I saw that other friend of yours, the dancer. I know him anyway. He's very good. I thought, maybe if I spoke to him, he could have a word with you. I don't know Louise. I've been going mad.'

'Henry, there are ways of getting in touch with me without sneaking about frightening everyone.'

'I know, I know. Will you forgive me, Louise?'

I look at him. It would be impossible to stay angry with Henry for long. He is so needy.

'You know, Louise, it's not your fault – Petra leaving me – it's not because of you. I think she was going to anyway.'

'What do you mean?'

'I mean, you mustn't blame yourself. She'd already decided before we came to see you. I think she came because she wanted to make sure that you were kosher. She had already decided to leave me and she wanted to make sure you would still be there for me. That's what she said anyway.'

'Hang on a minute. Are you saying that Petra just lied her way through that last session? I don't believe it.'

'Neither could I, but that's what she said. She left me a note. But it's not your fault, Louise. You weren't to know.'

Now I really am angry. It seems that everything I've been thinking about my clients, about the stalker, the letters . . . all of it was an illusion. I don't know anything. Everyone's been going quietly bonkers behind my back.

I go over to reception and ask if I can see Kevin.

When I find Kevin's cubicle the curtains are drawn and there's nobody else around. I clear my throat.

'Kevin?'

No reply.

'Kevin?' I say, a little louder. Still nothing.

I peel back a handful of curtain. Kevin is lying in a foetal position with his back to me.

'Kevin, it's me, Louise.' He moves his head, slowly and sees me. He smiles.

'I knew you'd come.'

'Are you badly hurt?'

'It's nothing. It's an old back injury. I deserve it.'

'Kevin . . .'

'It's all right, Louise. You don't have to say anything. You weren't to know. It's all my fault. I shouldn't have been there. I thought he was going to hurt you. I saw your boyfriend go out and I knew you were all alone. I didn't trust him.'

'But Kevin . . . oh, it's unbearable,' I shake my head in confusion.

'Louise, it's me. It's not you. I always do this. I mess everything up. I'm to blame.'

'Kevin, that's no good. It's no good just wiping everything out by saying you're to blame. It takes more than one person to create a mess like this. You can't just go through your life ignoring the things that really matter.'

'Like you?'

I look at him. He is very pale, but trying to smile.

'Oh Kevin,' I sigh. We stay like this for a while, Kevin trying not to show his vulnerability, me staring at him, feeling such a fool.

He holds out his hand and I take it.

'Louise, I know right now I must seem like the most stupid and pathetic man on earth . . .'

'Yes.'

'Okay. I am the most stupid and pathetic . . . I'm not always like this. It's something in me. Something I was born with. But I'm not all bad.'

'I know that, Kevin.'

'Can I talk to you, honestly? Now that we're outside the clinic?'

'Of course.'

'I mean as a friend. I want you to be my friend.'

'I am your friend, Kevin. I care about you.'

'Do you? Do you really?' The glimmer of a tear sparkles at the corner of his eye. I look away.

'Look, this might not be the best time to talk, you know . . .'

'It's okay. I want to tell you, Louise. I want to explain myself. I want you to know what I've been going through.'

I smile at him. Poor Kevin with his infernal emotional wrestling.

'I don't expect you to forgive me, Louise. And I don't expect you to like me anymore,' he pauses and looks pleadingly into my eyes. 'But you did like me once, didn't you? Just for a while?'

'Yes, Kevin.'

'You see, I thought it was you. When I first met you, you had that same thing that my father saw in my mother. That same appearance. As if you were apart from other people, spiritual, somehow. Meant to be,' he pauses, looking uncomfortable.

'I knew straightaway, Louise, the first time I came to the clinic. I knew something would happen between us.'

'Well, then why did you back away, Kevin?' I have a lump in my throat. 'Why did you run out like that?'

'Because it wasn't right, Louise. You knew that. Not there, not like that. Not with that reception woman listening. We were meant to be together somewhere beautiful, Louise. Somewhere perfect . . .'

'Another world, maybe.'

'Yes. Probably.'

There is a lull.

A nurse pokes her head round the curtain.

'Ah, Mrs Ryan?'

'No. No, I'm a friend.'

'Doctor's ready to take a look now. Would you mind waiting

in reception? Someone will be along soon to tell you what's happening. All right, Kevin?'

Kevin hardly notices. He looks barely conscious. I don't get to see him again that night.

I hang about in reception for a while. Then I call a cab. Malcolm is waiting for me when I get home.

'Darling, are you all right? I've been so worried. I called the hospital. Where the fuck have you been?'

I don't answer, I just bury my head in his strong warm chest and he holds me.

'Tim's in bed,' he says softly after a while. 'Come on, let's get you a drink and get you upstairs.' I nod.

'Was it really horrible?' I nod again. 'My poor darling. And I thought dancers were the worst drama queens.' This makes me smile. 'That's better. Now what can I do to make you feel better? Hmmm?' I shrug.

'I know just the thing,' he says.

He takes me upstairs to the bedroom and peels off my clothes. I lie face down on the bed and Malcolm proceeds to deliver the most thorough, liquifying massage. He even does my leg muscles and ankles and all over my arms down to my finger joints. And he talks all the time. Slow, romantic thoughts about us. Me and him looking after each other until we're old. Me and him being twin souls. Me and Malcolm taking on the world and setting it alight. Because we know how to love.

twenty-five

THE STORM HAS CLEARED the air. On Friday afternoon I decide to walk to the hospital.

Kevin is sitting up in bed looking decidedly better. He smiles. A warm, knowing smile.

'Florence Nightingale,' he says.

'Hardly,' I sit on the chair by his side. But Kevin pats the bed.

'Please?' then he holds out his hand. 'Friends?'

'Of course we're friends, Kevin,' I give him my hand and sit up on the bed. He kisses my knuckles. 'I brought peaches. Oh and a book. Here.'

'Thank you. Ah, Pushkin. I'll take that as a compliment. You decided to steer clear of metaphysics then?'

'I thought you might need a little diversion.'

'You thought right. I can read meanings into anything, Louise. But you know that, don't you?'

'Kevin . . .'

He puts a finger to my lips to stop me. It's an adult move.

'It's all right. It's me who should talk. So, you've finally worked it out. I know you don't believe in apologies – it's not part of the therapeutic ethos, is it? But I will say sorry, because I am. It was all my mistake. I . . . I've never met anyone like you before,

Louise. And I really did think for a moment that it was you,' Kevin's hand strokes my face and comes to rest on my shoulder.

'But that's not why I've been following you. Spying on you, I suppose you'd call it. Actually I only did that because I felt that you were in danger. There is a connection between us, you see.'

'But I wasn't in danger, Kevin. I can look after myself.'

'No, Louise. You can't. You need that man.' I sigh, loudly. I haven't come here for a lecture.

'I know you think I'm a pain, but I do know what I'm talking about. You need him and he needs you. I was very confused at first. I never went to Ireland at Easter. You know that, don't you? That's when I started following you. Just to keep an eye on you. I saw you go home with him. I waited outside for hours in a cab. When I saw you come out I sent him on to pick you up. Remember the minicab? I was worried about you, spending the night with a man who . . . well, I've never come across anyone quite like it. I find that threatening, you know. It's threatening because of what it says about people like me. It's we who are the specimens – relics. We've lost.'

'Kevin. It's not a competition.'

'That's exactly what it is. But it's okay. I've seen how happy he makes you. I'm back in my own corner now. I had a visit last night from a woman. A woman that I really love.'

I smile.

'So, I might not be needing your professional help anymore, Louise,' Kevin holds my hand. 'That's good, isn't it? That means you've won.'

'It wasn't a battle, Kevin. And yes, it is good.'

'You may not realise it, Louise, but you've helped me enormously. It's all because of you. I never had a problem with S. E. X. But you knew that, didn't you? That wasn't the problem at all.'

'So, how did I help?'

'You showed me how to love, Louise. When I saw you with your man, it made me realise what you'd been trying to explain to me. That it's not about perfection. It's not about achieving a goal. It's not even about finding your match.'

'What is it about, then?'

'It's about giving. It's about finding someone who needs what you've got to give. And giving it to them. That's what you're doing, isn't it, Louise? Isn't that what you were trying to teach me? I didn't realise you were just doing your job. Very cleverly. I am sorry, Louise. I hope I haven't made you hate me.'

'Of course not.'

We both look elsewhere for a few moments. This is all rather surreal. Then I find the courage to ask, 'Why did you send those letters?'

Kevin groans and turns his face away, into the pile of pillows. I wait.

When he lifts his face again he is grinning. That Kevin grin. I can't return it.

'They were disturbing, Kevin.'

'I know, I know. I'm sorry. What can I say? I was confused. I'm a fool, Louise, compared to you. I don't understand the things you understand. I thought, I honestly thought you were in danger. I wanted to stop you seeing them. All those men — strange and dangerous men. I just wanted you to see me. Me. It was stupid. I realise that now. You weren't frightened, were you, Louise? I couldn't bear to think I'd upset you.'

'Well, they weren't exactly pleasant reading.'

'Oh I know, I know. Just put it down to temporary insanity. Can you? Can you forgive me?'

'Kind of.'

'Bless you.'

We fall silent again. I guess this is the end of the story as far as Kevin and I are concerned. He's pushing me away. Which is a good sign.

'Well, I should go. Things to do, you know.'

'Yes, of course. Thank you for coming. It's good to know that you care,' he gives me a look.

'Yes, Kevin, I do. We're not made of stone, you know.'

'That's good.'

'I suppose you won't be coming anymore, then? To the clinic.'

'I hope not. I . . . I am sorry, Louise . . . about the other day. I didn't mean to embarrass you.'

'Forget it. It's my job.'

'Yes, of course.'

'Well, I'll come and see you again, if you like.'

'I should be out of here some time today. It's nothing. Just an old back injury. They've taken X-rays, but there's nothing new.'

'Oh good.'

'I'll be in touch, Louise. Soon.'

I get up to go. 'Okay.'

'And I'll return this book. I know how you hate to lose books.'

'See you then,' I bend down and kiss him on the cheek and then I walk away without looking back. I feel like crying.

But once out in the sunshine I suddenly feel extraordinarily happy. Everything is clear. It is hot and beautiful. I walk uphill to the National Trust House which has the most serene gardens. Lying on the grass by the pond, listening to the birds and the delighted screams of a little child playing with a dog, I thank Kevin. He's given me something back. It's that childlike quality of his. That naivety. Or maybe the opposite. And it's the beginning of the weekend.

twenty-six 26

MALCOLM'S SHOW IS AMAZING. I don't understand it all, but it's beautiful and sad, and moments of it are extraordinarily violent. Timmy is gripped. He decides he wants to be a dancer.

We hang about afterwards, waiting for them to get changed. Claire appears first and we have obligatory hugs. Then Paul, miraculously fighting fit for the first night, then some of the others. They make a bit of a fuss over Timmy and Gerard so when Malcolm comes sheepishly into the room, not lifting his face and heading straight for the bar, I am the first person to spot him.

'Darling . . .' I start.

'Don't. Please don't do any of that obsequious shit. Just tell me whether you liked it or not and then let's talk about something else.'

'Like it? I was . . . I was . . .'

'Bored?'

'No. God no. I was . . . elevated. It was very moving. I don't think I've ever seen anything like it.'

He lifts his face gradually and I can see he is smiling.

'Really?'

'Really.'

'Thank you.' He kisses me on the lips and a whoop goes up from the others. They are about to get very drunk very quickly.

I make my excuses and take the boys home, promising Malcolm a hero's welcome when he arrives.

By the time he does get home, I've sat for several hours trying to put together a clear first proposal for changing the focus of the clinic to work with offenders. I've also decided that I will definitely marry him.

He's nearly paralytic when he gets home, clutching a number of bouquets from admirers. There's no show tomorrow so he has a day of rest. He needs it.

We lounge around all the next day, talking about the show and Malcolm answers numerous phonecalls from people telling him how marvellous he is.

When Timmy comes home he persuades Malcolm to teach him some steps and I escape to the bath for some reflection. I seem to have everything. Career, lover, family . . . but something is niggling at me. And it won't let go.

When Timmy's gone to bed and after a few glasses of wine I broach the subject, tentatively.

'Do you think you would ever want to get married?'

'Only to you.'

'But would you?'

'Well, there's not much point in talking about what I want, is there? I know your views on marriage.'

'Do you? Why don't you ask?'

'What are your views on marriage?'

'No. I mean, why don't you ask me?'

'What?'

'To marry you.'

'Because you'd say no.'

'Would I? Try me.'

'Will you marry me?'

'Yes.'

'Oh my God. You mean it?'

'Do you?'

'Yes. I think so.'

'Well then. So do I.'
'Wow . . .'

twenty-seven

SO, WE'RE GOING TO GET married. I can't stop smiling. Life suddenly seems so simple.

I don't see Kevin again. There's a hole in my appointment diary for Thursday afternoons. On Friday a parcel arrives for me; my John Donne, my Pushkin and another plain, hardbacked notebook. There's a card with it – a picture of the monastery at Glendalough and a scrawled message.

'Thought you might be missing me, so I've sent you a memento. Read it when you're happy. God bless. Kevin.'

I open the book.

KEVIN'S DIARY

It is four months since I met you, Louise. I am writing this for you. It will be a record of our relationship. For our children.

I love you. I have known that from the beginning. If I go back I can remember how it was. Everything. Can you?

Entry 1: January
I have met her. Now I am sure. There have been false alarms before. But now I know. There can be no mistaking this. The way she looks at me. The way she anticipates my thoughts. I feel

I know her, even though I don't. This is that dreamed of meeting, that long awaited mystery. Question and answer.

Don't mistake me, Louise, little one, or whoever you are reading this. I don't mean this is the end. I mean, this is the moment I have longed for. I knew as soon as I walked in the building, for a stupid bet – a cynical joke – I knew. I was blind and now I see. Thanks to you, Louise.

I have never been to a prostitute before. Louise is not a prostitute. She is a sex therapist, which is different. I have girlfriends. In fact, I date women all the time. But I have never really enjoyed it. Which is why my 'mates' set me up with this appointment. They say the day they come home – we share a · house, three of us – and find me snogging a girl on the sofa, they will believe in God, or eat their hats, or something, anyway.

So, I came to see you. To prove that I am not afraid of sex. I came to see you, Louise, an expert. To make them eat their hats.

Enough about me.

You are the most beautiful woman I have ever seen. Cliché. You are quite old. I mean, not young. You have lines on your face, but they are happy, smiling lines. Your figure is not perfect, but breathtaking nonetheless. You are confident. But shy when you meet me. I notice the change. You have a striding manner, but with me, you go soft. You knew me, as soon as I walked in. Like I knew you.

The weirdest thing is that I knew before I even opened the diary – I knew what the handwriting would look like. It's that joined up writing. The same as the note asking me to marry him. The note that I found in a leaflet for Malcolm's show ... in my flat ... on my kitchen table. I don't want to imagine how he did it.

I flick through the diary and find a passage several pages from the end.

Entry 22

Have you seen me? Do you know where I hide to watch you?

I know you are unhappy. I think you may find yourself like I have if you open your heart to love. A love that was meant to be. I do not expect you to love me because I am your dream come true – I know there are thousands of men more attractive, more amenable, more your-kind-of-guy – but God has sent us to each other, Louise. And we must love each other until we die.

And I do want you. Don't be deceived by the gentleman in me.

Louise. I desire you. I dream of you. You are a very powerful woman. That is why you must not let them take it away from you. That is why you need me. I know you.

I put it down for a minute and try to conjure up a picture of Kevin in my mind. I can see his smile, his lovely, intense, blue eyes. I can smell his aftershave.

I turn to the back page.

It was always you, Louise. When you came to the hospital today I knew I could not live without you.

I love you. It is a feeling like nothing I have ever known. It is not calm or uplifting like the love of Jesus. It is insistent, necessary as a heartbeat.

So the rest, Louise, you will have to write alone.

God bless.

x

Transfixed, I touch the pages of the diary; a schoolboy's note-book. It makes me smile and I can see Kevin's face, grinning back at me. Tolerant, charming, good-looking and solvent. Poor Kevin.

Also published by Serpent's Tail

Ameena Meer

Bombay Talkie

'An exuberant comedy of the often painful meeting of Indian and Western manners' *Sunday Times*

'Feisty, sexy, moving, as if Merchant-Ivory swallowed *The Face*' *New Statesman & Society*

'A new kid on the literary block who is not afraid to ask questions and does not shirk her responsibility in aiming the answers, with empathy and affection, right between your eyes' *Asian Times*

Sabah, a young American woman, sets out to discover her identity and heritage in India, only to stumble into a demimonde of decadently upper-class Indians. Meanwhile, her ageing Bombay movie-star uncle and his formerly docile wife search through London and New York for their lovelorn gay son.

Across three continents, arranged marriages bursting at the seams, and all the glitz of Bollywood, *Bombay Talkie* is the story of people whose lives span several cultures, but who don't quite belong in any of them. Through this complex family saga, Ameena Meer sends up stereotypes of East and West with irony, wit and compassion.

Diane Langford

Left for Dead

Montse Letkin works for the council. She's what you might call a snooper. Montse is getting so good at her job that her boss Gwendoline Rhodes – that's the one they used to call Red Gwen – has lined Montse up as her personal security consultant. Montse wasn't so good at that though – Gwendoline fell out of a high window. And it would suit a lot of people if Montse took the rap.

In Montse Letkin, Diane Langford has created a heroine of our times, a bruised and cynical young woman learning the hard way that the personal really is political.

Left For Dead is a taut thriller set in London about ten minutes into the future. In a city where privatisation is the watchword and politics a dirty word. In a city where the weak and the homeless had best fend for themselves. In a city of secrets and lies, legacies collide in an unsettling, visionary slice of millennial noir.

Daniel Evan Weiss

Honk If You Love Aphrodite

Written in the epic style of Homer's *Odyssey, Honk If You Love Aphrodite* is the story of one man's quest to return across modern-day New York City to the woman he adores. Aphrodite, the goddess of love, sends her son to deliver this mortal Stanley from many perils: the trials of life in the subway and the underworld below it; an enchanting Voodoo dancer; a drug dealer whose turf Stanley transgresses; women with fervid desire for his attentions.

The greatest obstacle is not the colorful mortals Stanley encounters, or even the gods of the modern world, but rather Stanley's own divided heart. Does he truly want to return to the woman, as he claims? It is the duty of the son of Aphrodite to find out before the dawn.

This swift, hilarious adventure sweeps the reader through the city, and ultimately through the many faces of love in our time. It confirms Daniel Evan Weiss as a writer with a profound understanding of the rules of attraction between men and women today.

Daniel Evan Weiss

The Swine's Wedding

When Allison Pennybaker and Solomon Beneviste announce their engagement, the trouble begins: the Pennybakers plan a church wedding they can't afford, while Solomon's mother traces the Beneviste genealogy all the way back to the Spanish Inquisition. Both sides take determined, unwitting steps to promote a disaster. In darkly comic mode, Daniel Evan Weiss has once again profound truths to say about the human condition – this time about marriages between Jews and Christians.

'Weiss' powerful message seems to be that obsession with the injustices of the past is no less dangerous than ignoring them, a valuable lesson in this age of identity-group politics and universal victimhood... *The Swine's Wedding* is a funny, dark and ultimately searing book that is both a pleasure to read and too painful to forget' *Newsday*

'Weiss does a fine job on the women, whose wit and originality convince and endear. His consistently light touch contrasts starkly with the scenes of horrifying torture used to illustrate past oppressions, yet perfectly conveys his point: that bitterly harking back to the ills of the past can be as damaging as forgetting them. Neat' *Time Out*

'If you've experienced the nightmare of wedding preparations, you'll wince at Weiss's brilliantly plotted, blackly funny horror story. If you haven't, this modern-day Romeo and Juliet tale may put you off for life' *Cosmopolitan*

Michel Houellebecq

Whatever

'No sex drive, no ambition, no real interests either . . . I consider myself a normal kind of guy. Well perhaps not completely, but who is completely, huh? Eighty per cent normal, let's say.'

Ever found yourself all at sea at work? Suffered from information overload?

If you have, Houellebecq's grim, funny and clever tongue-in-cheek exploration of corporate jargon, psychobabble and the ineffectual use of long words is for you.

Just thirty, with a well-paid job and no love-life, our narrator smokes four packs of cigarettes a day and writes weird animal stories – cows and all – in his spare time. He's tolerably content in his boredom – until he's packed off with the unimaginably ugly Raphael Tisserand to train provincial servants in the use of a new computer system . . .

'Officially, then, I'm in a depression. The formula seems a happy one to me. It's not that I feel tremendously low; it's rather that the world around me appears high.'

A smash hit in France, *Whatever* made Michel Houellebecq, poet, essayist and cultural commentator, the spokesperson for a new generation. Free from the baggage of history, Houellebecq has found a sarcastic and witty voice with which to capture the rituals of daily life, to articulate the vanishing freedom of a world over-determined by science.

'A glittering study of disaffection, half caustic and half uproarious'
Robert Winder